P9-CQE-186

The Larkville Legacy

A secret letter…two families changed forever.

Welcome to the small town of Larkville, Texas, where the Calhoun family has been ranching for generations.

Meanwhile, in New York, the Patterson family rules America's highest echelons of society.

Both families are totally unprepared for the news that they are linked by a shocking secret. For hidden on the Calhoun ranch is a letter that's been lying unopened and unread—until now!

Meet the two families in all 8 books of this brand-new series:

The Cowboy Comes Home by Patricia Thayer

Slow Dance with the Sheriff by Nikki Logan

Taming the Brooding Cattleman by Marion Lennox

The Rancher's Unexpected Family by Myrna Mackenzie

His Larkville Cinderella by Melissa McClone

The Secret that Changed Everything by Lucy Gordon

The Soldier's Sweetheart by Soraya Lane

The Billionaire's Baby SOS by Susan Meier

Dear Reader,

I was excited when my editor invited me to participate in The Larkville Legacy, an eight-book continuity series centred around two families, a secret and a ranch in Larkville, Texas. I've read many romances set on ranches, but I had never written one. I figured it was time. Imagine my surprise when I discovered the hero in my book wasn't a cowboy but a famous movie star! And the story doesn't take place in Texas, either.

Megan Calhoun, the youngest of the Calhoun siblings, is an aspiring costume designer. She's interning on a film set in Hollywood, far away from friends, family and Larkville. The last person she expects to befriend her is Adam Noble, a handsome stuntman turned leading man.

Setting a story at a movie studio (aka "the lot") and in the world of filmmaking was fun, but it offered a few challenges.

The first was Megan's costume designer occupation. My family says I'm "fashion-challenged." I prefer to say I dress for comfort. One of the perks of being a writer! Fortunately a friend is a designer and Irish dance dressmaker. Knowing her and how she works gave me some much-needed insight into my heroine.

The second challenge was my lack of moviemaking knowledge. Thankfully a friend from college, who lives in the Los Angeles area and has worked on films, offered not only to help me but also to put me in contact with a producer and a costume designer, who were happy to answer my many questions.

I hope you enjoy Megan and Adam's story and The Larkville Legacy series.

Melissa

MELISSA McCLONE

His Larkville Cinderella

HARLEQUIN®
entertain, enrich, inspire™

Recycling programs
for this product may
not exist in your area.

ISBN-13: 978-0-373-17842-1

HIS LARKVILLE CINDERELLA

First North American Publication 2012

Copyright © 2012 by Harlequin Books S.A.

Special thanks and acknowledgment are given to Melissa McClone for her contribution to The Larkville Legacy series.

This edition published by arrangement with Harlequin Books S.A.

For questions and comments about the quality of this book, please contact us at CustomerService@Harlequin.com.

® and TM are trademarks of Harlequin Enterprises Limited or its corporate affiliates. Trademarks indicated with ® are registered in the United States Patent and Trademark Office, the Canadian Trade Marks Office and in other countries.

www.Harlequin.com

Printed in U.S.A.

With a degree in mechanical engineering from Stanford University, the last thing **Melissa McClone** ever thought she would be doing was writing romance novels. But analyzing engines for a major U.S. airline just couldn't compete with her "happily-ever-afters." When she isn't writing, caring for her three young children or doing laundry, Melissa loves to curl up on the couch with a cup of tea, her cats and a good book. She enjoys watching home decorating shows to get ideas for her house—a 1939 cottage that is *slowly* being renovated. Melissa lives in Lake Oswego, Oregon, with her own real-life hero husband, two daughters, a son, two lovable but oh-so-spoiled indoor cats, and a no-longer-stray outdoor kitty that has decided to call the garage home.

Melissa loves to hear from her readers. You can write to her at P.O. Box 63, Lake Oswego, OR 97034, USA, or contact her via her website, www.melissamcclone.com.

Books by Melissa McClone

IT STARTED WITH A CRUSH…
FIREFIGHTER UNDER THE MISTLETOE
EXPECTING ROYAL TWINS!
NOT-SO-PERFECT PRINCESS

Other titles by this author available in ebook format.

For Alison Thrasher

Special thanks to Julie Adams,
Mary Church, Roxanne Coyne,
Jay at Zuma Jay Surfboards in Malibu,
Terri Reed and Jennifer Shirk.

CHAPTER ONE

MALIBU, California, was a long way from her family's ranch in Larkville, Texas.

Tension bunched Megan Calhoun's shoulder muscles. She would be impressed with the exclusive gated beach community if she weren't under so much pressure. She exited her car, parked on the driveway of a beachfront mansion. The breathtaking Mediterranean-inspired villa belonged to an award-winning film producer.

A breeze rustled the palm tree fronds. Gray clouds made it look more like winter than springtime, but the temperature was warm. Or maybe she was working so hard she didn't have time to feel cold.

Interning for a film costume designer in Hollywood was supposed to be a dream come true. So far this first week on the job had been nothing but sixteen-hour-long days filled with driving, picking up and delivering things and running countless other "errands."

Intern and *indentured servant* seemed to mean the same thing with production to begin next week. Sleep was now considered optional. If this was life before filming, she couldn't imagine what working on an actual movie set would be like.

She jammed her car keys into the front pocket of her jeans, then grabbed the large leather portfolio from the backseat of her car. Eva Redding, the woman who held the fate of Megan's internship and possibly her future career, had left the studio this morning with the wrong portfolio. That delayed a meeting with a couple of Hollywood's heavy hitters. Now everyone was waiting for Megan to arrive with the correct designs so they could continue discussing costume concerns with the proper visuals.

Hurrying toward the villa's entryway, her comfortable tennis shoes felt more like cement blocks encasing her feet.

No way would she let her nervousness about coming face-to-face with the producer and director get the best of her.

Failure wasn't an option. She was not returning to Larkville. Her family might be there, but no one else. Not even Rob Hollis, her best friend for as long as she could remember; he had taken an engineering job in Austin, Texas. Her fingers tightened around the portfolio.

She stepped onto a large, tiled entryway. In the corner, a green leafy potted plant stood as tall as her. A hanging vine with fuchsia flowers scented the air. A wrought-iron tiered shelf held terra-cotta pots filled with various flowering plants.

What if film costume design wasn't where she belonged, either? Her stomach churned as uncertainty threatened to get the best of her.

No. She had a job to do. Megan's father had always told her to do the best job possible no matter what.

She felt a pang of grief. If only her dad were here so he could give her a much needed confidence boost. She took a deep breath to calm herself and jabbed her finger against the doorbell.

As melodic, multitoned chimes rang inside the villa, she remembered the instructions given to her by the costume supervisor.

"Hand Eva the portfolio and get out of there without saying a word."

That would be no problem. Megan excelled at being silent and fading into the background. She'd been doing it most of her life. She'd never fit in at the ranch. Her dad had been the only one who seemed to get her and really care, but he was…gone.

A lump burned in her throat. Her dad, the larger than life Clay Calhoun, had died of pneumonia in October, seven months ago. She was on her own in more ways than one now.

The ten-foot-tall wooden door opened.

"About time." Eva snatched the portfolio away. In her early forties with a flawless ivory complexion and jet-black hair styled into a French twist, the woman wore a black tunic, pants and heels. African-inspired jewelry added a funky and unexpected twist to the stylish and elegant clothing. "What took you so long?"

On Megan's second day in Tinseltown, she'd learned one of the only acceptable answers for being late. "Traffic."

Her boss's hard, assessing gaze ran the length of Megan. Eva's red-glossed lips pursed with disapproval. "You're slouching. Stand straight."

Megan did.

"Is this how you dress on the ranch?"

A plain pink T-shirt, faded capri jeans and comfy tennis shoes weren't going to put Megan on any of Hollywood's best-dressed lists. But her clothing wouldn't draw any attention to her, either. Well, except for now. But she imagined nothing she wore would live up to Eva's exacting expectations. "Yes."

The word *ma'am* sat on the tip of Megan's tongue. She'd used the term with Eva on Monday, the first day of the internship. Megan wouldn't make that mistake again.

"I don't suppose you have any other clothes in your car," Eva said.

Megan had grown up on a ranch in middle-of-nowhere Texas and graduated college less than two weeks ago. All her clothing was casual except for a few of her own creations she'd never had any reason—or courage—to wear outside her bedroom. Not after being made fun of freshman year at high school for the way she'd dressed. After that happened she'd adopted Rob's and his friends' geek look as her own style. "No."

"Then let's go." Eva motioned her inside. "Everyone's out on the patio."

Panic rocketed from the brown hair piled on top of Megan's head to the tips of her canvas sneakers. She wasn't supposed to speak, but she wasn't supposed to stay, either. "I'm, uh, supposed to head back to the studio."

"Not anymore."

The cartwheels turning in her stomach would have made Larkville High's Cheer Team proud. Not that any of those girls had ever given Megan the time of day except when they were trying to fundraise for new uniforms or a competition. "My car…"

"…isn't going anywhere without you," Eva said. "Come on."

Megan stepped inside the villa. The door closed behind her with a thud.

Goose bumps covered her skin.

Trapped, except she wasn't standing in some dark, musty, Gothic manor. This mansion was bright with big windows and gleaming floors. The air smelled fresh, flowery with a hint of citrus. The temperature was cooler than outside. Air-conditioning. That explained the goose bumps.

Glancing around the foyer, she pressed her lips together to keep her mouth from gaping in awe. To the right, an elaborate wrought-iron chandelier hung over a huge dining table that seated twenty. The living room on the left was filled with expensive furnishings and fancy artwork with huge windows that showed the breathtaking ocean view.

Eva strode across the gleaming wood floor at a rapid clip, an amazing feat considering the high heels on her shoes. "Don't dawdle."

Megan quickened her pace. She had no idea what was going on. Pretty much if it wasn't illegal or immoral, she would do what was asked of her. Anything to secure a full-time position.

Eva glared back. "Don't talk unless someone addresses you directly."

Megan nodded. That suited her fine.

She followed her boss through glass doors out onto a massive deck overlooking the beach and ocean. A breeze carried the salty scent of the sea. The sky looked like yards of gray flannel spread out to the horizon.

The patio stretched across the backside of the house and was decorated as nicely as the interior. Seating arrangements had been set up with comfy pillow-covered chairs and chaise longues. One corner had a built-in barbecue and a bar with stools. There was even a hot tub.

Two men, who she didn't know, sat at a table. Both wore light-colored short-sleeved shirts, slacks and dark sunglasses even though the sky was overcast.

Another man and woman, both wearing sunglasses also, stood at the railing. She recognized them from the wardrobe department. The man looked all business in his dark, tailored pants, white long-sleeved dress shirt and multicolored silk tie. The cut and line of the woman's salmon-pink above-the-knee skirt and cap-sleeved jacket reminded Megan of a designer from Milan she'd written a paper on at college.

No one acknowledged her presence. Megan wasn't offended or surprised. Invisible could be her middle name.

Most people had been calling her "hey, you" or "new intern" since she arrived at the studio on Monday morning. She was, in a word, forgettable. Nothing special, as her late mother continually reminded Megan, whereas her three siblings—Holt, Nate and Jess—defined the word. Megan wondered if their new two half siblings, the Patterson twins, fathered by her dad before he married her mom, were more like Megan's brothers and sister than her.

"I finally have the designs." Eva's tone made the delay sound like Megan's fault. "We can get started now."

"Hey, you," a male voice said. "Girl in the pink T-shirt."

Megan looked at one of the men sitting at the table. He was handsome in a distinguished-gentleman sort of way. His tan skin and sun-bleached hair made her think he spent a lot of time outside. She guessed he might be the producer who lived here.

"Go get Adam," the man said.

Adam? The blood rushed from Megan's head. She had no idea who the guy was talking about.

Eva laughed. "Megan is new in town, Chas. She's from Texas and my latest intern. One of her former professors is a very close friend of mine who has an eye for raw talent. Emphasis on *raw*."

The man and woman standing at the rail looked at Megan for a nanosecond, then returned to their conversation.

Megan tried to let it roll off her. The way she used to do back in Larkville.

Here in Hollywood, she had no choice. Getting your foot in the door was all about connections. A few people managed positions on their own, but it wasn't easy. Professor Talbott had secured this internship for her. But nothing was guaranteed. She would have to prove her worth or she would find herself back at the ranch before the annual Fall Festival in October. Who was she kidding? She might be home by Fourth of July, or worse, Memorial Day.

A heavy weight pressed down on her. She struggled not to let her shoulders droop.

"Texas, huh?" the blond man Eva had called Chas said.

Megan nodded.

He gave her the once-over, but with his sunglasses on she couldn't tell what he thought about her. "Dallas or Austin?"

"Larkville."

"Never heard of it."

"You're not missing anything unless you like pickup trucks, cowboys and the smell of cow manure," she replied.

Her comment drew a wide smile full of straight, white teeth. "Sounds like lyrics to a country song."

"Megan," Eva said sharply. "Run down to the water. Tell Adam it's time for him to join us. That's Adam Noble, our star actor. I'm sure even a small-town Texas girl like you knows who he is."

Megan had seen some of his movies, action-adventure flicks that required him to take off his shirt as many times as possible. Adam had a killer, athletic body still toned from his college quarterback days and a classically handsome face. The guy also had a habit—perhaps a hobby—of having flings with his leading ladies. Or so the grocery store tabloids reported.

She nodded.

Most women would call the actor hot, but she preferred guys who were more…cerebral. Guys like her best friend, Rob. Her Mr. Right, if ever one existed. All she had to do was wait it out until he realized she was his Ms. Right.

A squawking noise sounded overhead. She looked up to see two seagulls. Their white feathers were almost lost against the cloudy sky. Very cool. She couldn't remember the last time she'd seen this type of bird.

"We don't have all day," Eva said.

Megan ran down the deck's staircase to the beach.

Eva's cackling laughter followed Megan onto the sand.

Her cheeks burned. Compassion and understanding didn't seem to exist in Hollywood. No one cared if she felt like the proverbial fish out of water, overwhelmed and exhausted. They only cared that she got the job done. If she couldn't, ten others were waiting to take her place.

Not. Going. To. Happen.

She would do whatever it took to succeed in this business. Not that she had seen any costume designs other than those hanging on the walls, storyboards and drafting tables at the work space at the studio. She'd touched only clothing and fabric bolts needed by the staff. But she knew how each coworker took their coffee or tea, what they ordered for lunch and that "Firebreather," Eva's nickname, wasn't an exaggeration.

Megan's tennis shoes sunk into the sand.

Her internship was nothing like she thought it would be. Girl Friday seemed too glorified a term for what she did. That was run errands, emphasis on the running. Gophers got more respect than she did. And she was doing this all for free…for the experience.

But paying her dues was required in the film industry.

Costume designers worked their way up in the food chain. She had to start somewhere. Whatever she was doing here was better than being stuck back in Larkville and using her sewing ability to make alterations at the nearest dry cleaners. If only Rob had wanted her to move to Austin instead of encouraging her to take this internship...

She stumbled over a piece of seaweed. Sticking her arms out to keep her balance, she managed to stay upright. No doubt she looked like an idiot. As usual. She was all limbs and hair. Always had been.

A few people stood at the water's edge. In spite of the gray sky, women wore tiny strips of fabric that showed off their toned and honey-gold tanned bodies. Megan would never have the nerve to wear a bikini like that even if the temperature had been warmer and the sun shining.

Men wore board shorts and no shirts. Muscular physiques abounded. One thing was certain. The beach was a magnet for attractive men. But she'd still take Rob over any of them, even if he were thinner with not so many muscles. He wanted to spend time with her. He was always there to give advice, offer support and hang out with. Guys like him were hard to find.

She looked at each of the men. None had Adam Noble's trademark tousled brown hair and loose curls.

Megan dug the toe of her shoe into the sand.

Where could he be?

She noticed everyone was looking at the water. A lone surfer rode a massive wave. He did a fancy move with his board. She thought he might wipe out, but he somehow stayed on his feet.

Two women cheered. Another clapped. One man whistled.

A different woman sighed. "Adam is so hot."

Megan studied the surfer, who wore some sort of wet suit. It didn't take her long to realize Adam Noble was the one riding the wave. He cut back and forth on his board, across the rolling wave, doing tricks and inspiring oohs-and-aahs from the captivated crowd.

Show-off.

She wasn't impressed. Okay, she would give him a few props for making the women drool and the men stare at him with envy. But Adam could have ridden the wave without doing so many risky moves. The guy had a starring role in a new feature film, one she would work on as part of her internship. He should be more careful, not out there endangering himself and possibly the entire production so he could perform for his adoring fans on such a big wave.

Talk about an idiot.

He reminded her of those cowboys back home who risked their lives for an eight-second ride on some bucking bull named Diablo. The guy was all brawn. He didn't have a brain cell in that handsome head of his.

No wonder his costars slept with him. They probably couldn't find anything to talk about with him and figured sex was an easy way to fill the time between scenes.

Thank goodness Adam was riding the wave to shore. The sooner she could get him to the villa, the sooner she would be able to get back to the studio.

Megan might be a lowly intern with only more errands to run, but she had better things to do than stand around and wait for a self-indulgent, stupid movie star like Adam Noble.

As Adam walked to the beach with his board tucked under his arm, waves lapped around his calves. Water dripped off his hair and ran down his lite three/two full suit. He couldn't wait until summer, his favorite season of the year, when he wouldn't need protection from the cold water.

He smiled at the small crowd watching him. Being a star meant putting up with fans wherever he went. He didn't mind. Fans were the ones who paid to see his movies. Without them, he'd still be doing stunts and going home with sore muscles and bruises.

He'd gotten used to the invasion of privacy except for the paparazzi. Those vultures lurked everywhere with their digital cameras and high-powered lenses, waiting for a chance to capture him looking or doing something stupid. He always had to be on guard and make everything he did appear effortless.

Like surfing.

Even if he thought he would wipe out. Twice.

Adam would hate to see a picture like that plastered over the internet and tabloid covers with a "shocking" headline blaming alcohol or drugs or some mysterious woman for his fall. The tabloids exaggerated and blew everything he did out of proportion. But not this time.

He'd stayed on his feet. Once again. And gotten a much needed rush. He loved surfing on the Fish, a light and maneuverable surfboard. Few things in this world beat taking a risk, whether it was with surfing or acting, and succeeding.

As he hit the sand, three women thrust out their chests barely covered by bikini tops and sucked in their stomachs.

His gaze ran along the line; the blonde had a pretty smile, the brunette had exotic looks and the auburn winked at him.

One thing he could say…his job didn't suck. But he wondered if any of the three women didn't use the word *like* in every other sentence and could have a conversation that lasted more than five minutes.

Men extended their arms to shake his hand. Other women said breathy hellos, tilted their heads coyly and touched his arm.

He continued through the crowd, acknowledging each person. Okay, the women. He preferred more of a challenge than many female fans offered, but he was still a man.

Nothing wrong with looking.

He could invite a couple women to Chas's villa, but he doubted the producer would want the meeting turned into a party. It had been delayed long enough due to the costume designs not being here. He should get back and see if they'd arrived.

His gaze left a zebra-striped bikini-clad *Sports Illustrated–* swimsuit-issue-worthy body and saw pink. He jerked to a stop so hard he thought he might get whiplash. Instead of soft skin and delectable cleavage, he saw a baggy pink T-shirt hiding every feminine curve he might want to check out. Jeans—baggy, as well—covered her legs except for white calves. Not the hint of a tan—or even a fake one—on her legs or arms.

Allergic to the sun? Unless she was one of those vampire types.

She looked to be in her early twenties. Her shoulders hunched, as if she were trying to hide or maybe had bad posture. Light brown unruly hair was clipped haphazardly on the top of her head. Corkscrew curly strands stuck out every which way. Unglossed lips pressed together in a thin line. But her eyes drew his attention.

Dark, thick lashes surrounded pretty brown eyes. The color reminded him of a cup of espresso. Dark and rich with subtle hints of something more, something deeper, spicier.

A funny feeling took root in his stomach.

He stared, captivated.

Warm, expressive…and not happy to see him.

He did a double take.

Disdain filled her eyes, making him feel like a piece of trash washed onto the sand by the tide. He knew the feeling all too well and didn't like it one bit.

Adam forced his feet to move and walked past her.

At least she wasn't one of those rabid stalker fans who stared at him in awe, saw his movies at least three times on opening weekends, slept on a pillowcase bearing his image and believed he was truly the character Neptune, his most successful role to date, and wanted him to impregnate her with a half human, half deity fetus. Those women scared him.

"Mr. Noble." A feminine voice with a slight twang called his name.

Adam stopped. People rarely called him mister. He kind of liked it. He wondered which of the scantily dressed beauties the Southern accent belonged to. He wouldn't mind playing Rhett Butler to a Scarlett O'Hara, especially one who showed the same strength as the Georgia belle. He turned.

The girl with the messy hair and pink T-shirt took a step toward him.

Her? He was usually luckier than that, except she did have beautiful eyes.

On second look, she wasn't as plain as he originally thought. She reminded him of a Midwestern tourist or one of those nerd types who attended schools like Cal Tech or MIT and recited lines from *The Lord of the Rings* without a moment's hesitation. Kind of cute if you liked geeks. "Yes?"

She looked at the sand, as if meeting his gaze would turn her into a block of stone. "The meeting is about to start. They would like you to come back to the, er, house."

Funny, but he would have never expected her to be in the business. She didn't look like any personal assistant he'd seen running around a lot or set. Someone's daughter or niece? Maybe the housekeeper or nanny. "You were sent to get me?"

As she nodded, hair fell out of the clip. Curly strands framed her face. Her high cheekbones, a nice straight nose and full lips were attractive. But she wore no mascara, eyeliner or foundation. Not a hint of lipstick. He was used to women wearing makeup and going to great lengths to play up their assets and look their best. This girl seemed to have missed that memo. Or maybe she didn't care what people thought about her. He found that idea very attractive.

"Duty calls, ladies," he said to the women in bikinis.

As they walked away with promising smiles, the girl before him shook her head. She'd yet to smile.

Her attitude amused him. He wondered what it would take to turn her disapproval into acceptance.

"Who are you? A PA?" Adam asked her.

She tilted her chin. "I'm Megan Calhoun. An intern."

Aha. So she was at the bottom of the food chain. But that didn't explain the way she was acting. Her attitude and her looks wouldn't help her move up the ladder.

"We should get going, then." He wanted to get her to crack

a smile. "I wouldn't want to be responsible for getting you into any trouble."

No smile, but her features relaxed. Gratitude shone in her eyes. "Thanks."

Interesting how she let every emotion show. The girl must never have heard the expression *poker face* before. Adam could have some fun with that. In fact, he would.

"You're welcome." He handed her his surfboard. "Here."

She inhaled sharply. As her fingers gripped the wet board, she struggled to hold on to it. The Fish weighed ten pounds or so, but it was half a foot taller than her. "You want me to carry this thing?"

The indignation in her voice made him bite back a smile. Not quite a modern-day Scarlett, but as close as he'd find on a beach in Malibu. "You're the intern."

"In costumes," she clarified.

Now that surprised him. Costume people tended to dress the part. They didn't wear their best clothes when working on the set because they could get dirty. But they usually looked good. Stylish, even in their grubbies. Megan dressed like one of the tech crew. Maybe she liked being comfortable, not stylish and fashionable.

"You're still an intern." Adam wanted to get a response out of her. This should do it. He grinned wryly. "And I'm the star."

CHAPTER TWO

MEGAN'S full lips narrowed into a thin line. Pink colored her cheeks. Resentful, offended, annoyed, angry, put out. Her feelings flashed across her face brighter than the neon lights on the Las Vegas Strip.

Adam had wanted a reaction. Looks like he got one.

He fought the urge to laugh. Someone who didn't know how to control her emotions was rare in a town where showing any weakness could mean you were shark bait. He liked it. "I suppose I can carry the board myself. If it's too much trouble for you."

Megan didn't say a word. But the determined set of her chin and the gold flames flickering in her eyes told him to back off.

He did. Playing with her was more fun than he thought it would be. He didn't want her to get angry and storm off. Not that any intern would do that if they had half a brain. Truth was, he was the star and could get away with...a lot.

She maneuvered the Fish awkwardly, as if she'd never held a surfboard before. Given the way she tried to carry it, she probably hadn't. She looked like she might tip over.

He reached toward her, but she shrugged off his assistance. Interesting. Many women liked playing the damsel in distress to his knight in shining armor. Not this one.

Megan readjusted the board, nearly losing her balance again. She walked toward the villa.

Adam's respect inched up. She was tougher than she looked.

He liked rooting for the underdog. He'd been one himself until recently.

He lengthened his stride to catch up to her. "Being an intern sucks. But you have to start somewhere in this business."

He waited for her to say something. She didn't.

"I was a stuntman and a stand-in before becoming an actor," he continued.

Still nothing. That was…odd.

Something had to be wrong with her. People sucked up to him no matter what he did. Women would kill to be in her spot right now. Not carrying the surfboard, but having his undivided attention.

"Long hours." Adam wasn't sure why he was trying so hard. Maybe because most women liked him, flirted with him, wanted him. He wasn't used to it when they didn't or how to feel about that. He settled on amused. A challenge was always nice. "But it paid off in the end."

Megan stared at Chas's patio about a hundred yards away, as if Adam didn't exist. He might as well be talking to a brick wall. That was both annoying and intriguing. Women didn't ignore him. Okay, a few did because they were playing hard to get. Megan didn't look like that type, but he'd never put anything past a woman. He'd grown up watching his mother do some crazy things to get a man.

"Let me guess," Adam said, not ready to give up. "You're interning in costumes, but you really want to be an actress."

Megan stared at him as if he were a wild animal let loose from its cage at the San Diego Zoo. A V formed above the bridge of her nose, making her look strangely attractive. "Do I look like someone who wants to be an actress?"

Her harsh tone matched the annoyance in her ·eyes. "Honestly, no. But you could be a method actor and deep in character at the moment."

The V deepened. "What character would that be?"

He studied her—curly, messy hair, slumping shoulders,

two-sizes-too-big clothes that could be hiding some delectable curves. Or not. "Insecure girl desperately seeking a boyfriend."

Her icy glare would have frozen the equator.

He'd been a little too honest. Next time he'd stick to being polite. "O-kay, not an actress."

As she walked—almost marched—away from him, heading toward Chas's place, Adam's curiosity grew. No rings on her fingers. Hooking up with her could be a possibility. Though she wasn't his type. He preferred athletic women who were tan, lithe and straight-to-bed sexy. Still he wouldn't forget those eyes anytime soon.

"So…" he said.

"I'm here doing my job, Mr. Noble," she said. "You don't have to go out of your way to talk to me."

Her straightforwardness surprised him.

"Call me Adam. I'm just messing with you about carrying my board. A little Hollywood hazing of the intern." He waited to see if she was amused. Nope. He almost regretted making her carry the board. "I'll take it now."

She tightened her grip on the board and sped up.

Stubborn. Adam had to admit he was impressed by Megan Calhoun's total lack of sucking up to him. He wanted to know more about her. "You sound like you're from the South."

No reply.

"You must be new in town," he tried again.

Megan glanced his way again, only this time her gaze was wary. "Why do you say that?"

Her pale skin and clothing were dead giveaways. Not to mention her ignoring him. Most people no matter what their job title and status in the industry would leech on to him, like barnacles on the hull of a boat, in hopes of getting a boost to their own careers. "Just a hunch."

"I've been here six days."

"A newbie."

She nodded.

"First time in Malibu?" he asked.

Another nod.

A breeze toyed with the ends of her hair. Adam wouldn't mind twisting one of those curls around his finger. He imagined her hair loose, flowing past her shoulders in long ringlets. The temptation to remove her hair clip was strong.

Nah, better not try it. She would drop the Fish. Or hit him with it. The mousy ones could be a lot stronger than they looked. Megan might not have the posture of a ballerina, but she was showing some backbone.

"They call this weather the May Gray," he explained. "The June Gloom follows."

"I thought the beach would be sunny."

"Don't let the clouds fool you, you can still get sunburned. Always wear sunscreen." That was what his mom had told him. He bet Megan's nose would be a little pink soon. Her cheeks, too. "How do you like Los Angeles?"

"I haven't seen much," she said. "No time."

It would be hard to sightsee and make friends with the hours interns worked. No pay. No sleep. Zero respect. "If you're ever lonely and want me to show you around town…"

The offer escaped before he realized what he was saying.

Her pursed full lips looked as if they'd been specially made for slow hot kisses. Maybe she would say yes. He wouldn't mind a kiss. He was curious whether she tasted sweet or bitter.

"Thanks," she said. "But I'm not that lonely."

Most likely bitter.

But her dismissive tone only piqued his interest. Chasing Megan could be interesting. Catching her, too. He winked. "At least not yet."

She stumbled.

Adam grabbed hold of her, wrapping an arm around her waist, and the surfboard, to keep both from hitting the sand. Her body tensed beneath his hand. "Relax. I've got you."

She stiffened more. "I'm okay now."

Better than okay, actually. He expected the baggy clothes to be hiding a soft, lumpy body. But that didn't seem to be the case. Megan Calhoun, intern, was full of surprises and much thinner and fitter than she looked. "Let go of the board."

"I'm fine."

"Let go or I won't let go of you."

Her hands released the board as if it were on fire.

He liked her doing what he said. Playful images of the things he wanted to tell her to do to him ran through his mind. He could think of a few ways to put a big smile on her face. He wondered how her eyes expressed attraction, desire, passion.

Megan accelerated her pace.

Adam kept up with her. "What's the hurry?"

"My boss is watching us."

He glanced up at the deck. Chas, who was producing Adam's new film, stood next to Eva Redding, the costume designer. Adam hadn't known which of the three costume people Megan would be working for, but she didn't seem the type to get along with Eva. Not that many people got along with her. "You're interning with Firebreather?"

Megan nodded.

Damn. Adam should have made the connection before. He still wasn't sure why he'd been included in today's costume meeting, but at least they'd told him to go surfing while they waited for the designs to arrive. He probably shouldn't have surfed for so long. He wanted to give his input and make this film the best it could be. Maybe then he'd get the recognition he wanted for his acting. "I'm sorry."

And he was. Not only for having Megan carry his board. Someone who wore her heart on her sleeve would never stand a chance with Firebreather. Eva Redding wowed people with her talent, but also intimidated them with her take-no-prisoners personality. She went through interns like bubble gum. Rumor had it the last one, a young woman he'd met during a costume fitting, was let go on her fourth day.

"When did your internship start?" he asked.

"Monday."

Three days ago. The clock was winding down for poor Megan.

Adam felt like a jerk for treating her the way he had. She must be under a lot of pressure. He hadn't made a great impression, either. Having Eva see him holding Megan could make things worse for the intern.

He knew what it was like to work your way up from the bottom. It would be hard enough to succeed with Eva Redding as a boss. He didn't want to do anything to screw up Megan's internship. Best to back off so she didn't get in trouble.

As Adam rinsed off in the villa's outdoor shower, Megan stood by the stairs with his surfboard, something he apparently called the Fish. She hadn't been sure what to do when they arrived at the house. She decided to wait for Adam, figuring it might be considered bad form to go up to the deck without him given he was "the star."

The guy had some nerve.

She was surprised he hadn't wanted her to walk four feet behind him, as if he were royalty. But Adam Noble was no Prince Charming. Not like Rob, who would never allow her to carry a shopping bag, let alone a surfboard. Well, if he surfed. Rob didn't like the water. He was into mental challenges, not physical ones.

Still she couldn't deny Adam's attractiveness. His eyes shone brightly and he could carry a conversation, suggesting he wasn't as stupid as she initially thought. But it was weird that a movie star of his caliber had bothered talking to her at all.

If you're ever lonely and want me to show you around town...

Yeah, right. The man had gorgeous half-naked women throwing themselves at him. No way would he want to spend time with someone like her.

Insecure girl desperately seeking a boyfriend.

Surprisingly he'd gotten it half right.

She might be insecure. Who wouldn't be in a brand-new

place doing a brand-new job and after a lifetime of being told she didn't fit in? But she wasn't looking for a boyfriend. Far from it.

She knew the man she wanted. All she needed was for her best friend to come to his senses and realize friendship was the perfect foundation for a serious, committed relationship. Marriage would follow. Then a dog, cat and kids. A happily ever after, the kind she'd grown up watching in the movies and dreamed about for years.

The shower stopped.

Adam's wet suit hung over the swinging door. Megan saw his bare feet underneath. He stepped into a pair of blue-and-white board shorts.

A lump formed in her throat. Had he not been wearing anything underneath the wet suit? Not that it mattered one way or the other.

The shower door swung open. Adam stepped out.

Her breath caught in her throat.

He wore board shorts. No shirt. His hair was wet—so was the rest of him.

She swallowed.

Water rolled off his wide shoulders, down his muscular arms and chest, past his six-pack abs to his narrow hips....

What in the world was she doing?

Heat flooded Megan's cheeks. She forced her gaze up to the patio. Eva no longer stood there. Thank goodness. Megan didn't want her boss to think she was ogling the film's star.

Yes, Adam Noble was handsome and had a killer body if you liked that all-American athletic look. But *she* would never be interested in *him*.

Adam sauntered over, his wet hair pushed back off his face. Water dripped from the ends.

Her pulse kicked up a notch. Maybe two. She understood why he'd been named one of the Fifty Most Beautiful People.

"Thanks." He took the surfboard from her. "After you."

She motioned him ahead of her. "They're not waiting for me."

Adam opened his mouth as if to speak, but didn't. He climbed the stairs. She followed.

On the patio, the others sat around the table. People greeted Adam. He gave each person his full attention, focusing his gaze on them, the way he'd done with her on the beach.

Her father had been called "larger than life." Adam Noble was like that, too. His charisma captivated people. Herself included.

Adam joined the five people at the table.

"Hey, you," Chas said to Megan. He motioned to the bar where a stainless-steel coffee carafe and several glass pitchers containing various colored beverages sat. "Refill everyone's drinks, Texas."

Megan cringed at the nickname. She wanted to forget where she was from. But Chas was the producer so she assumed that meant he could call her what he wanted. Given the choice, she preferred "hey, you" to "Texas."

She headed to the bar, resigning herself to the fact her internship wouldn't give her much costume design experience, but she'd end up with great waitress and driving skills. She picked up the requisite pitchers and refilled the glasses on the table.

"We are on schedule." Eva had the costume sketches displayed. She must have started the meeting without Adam. "Based on our last meeting, Damon, I made the alterations to Calliope's costumes. I'll need Krystal and Adam for a final fitting, then we'll be ready to shoot."

Megan had loved Krystal Kohl's most recent movie. The tall, willowy and gorgeous actress was so talented. Though Krystal had a reputation for being difficult on the set and everywhere else.

Adam held one of the sketches. "This is the new gown for the dinner scene."

Eva nodded. "Krystal will look divine next to you in the Dior tuxedo."

He nodded. "Excellent work."

Eva's sincere smile made her look nice. Maybe there was more to the designer than her bright red lipstick and severe personality. "Thank you, Adam."

Chas removed his sunglasses. "Great work, Eva. As usual."

Damon nodded. "That's exactly the look I was going for. And I appreciate the effort you put into the new designs, but there's been a slight change. That's why we've asked all of you here today."

Eva's gaze bounced between the producer and director like a Ping-Pong ball during a championship match. "Define *slight change*."

Chas leaned forward. "Krystal Kohl is at a rehab facility in Tucson. Her role is being recast."

No one gasped. No one said a word, but an uncomfortable silence fell over the table.

Eva stared at the costume designs with a blank face.

The two wardrobe people looked at each other, but their expressions didn't change.

Megan stood at the bar arranging glasses and pitchers, trying to appear disinterested. She might be a "newbie," as Adam had called her, but this couldn't be good news with filming scheduled to start next week.

She looked at Adam to see his reaction.

His posture hadn't changed. He sipped from his glass of water, as if the news of his leading lady being replaced at the last minute wasn't a big deal. It didn't seem to be except...

A muscle pulsed at his jaw.

Not as immune as the others appeared to be. He wasn't happy about the role being recast.

"A lot of work went into casting Krystal as Calliope," Adam said. "This isn't some summer blockbuster flick, but a serious drama."

Chas nodded. "We know the caliber of talent needed for the role."

Adam leaned back in his chair. "Who are you thinking about as a replacement?"

"Lane Gregory," Damon said. The award-winning actress was the only child of two movie stars and America's sweetheart. "We've worked together before. Very professional. She can step in at the last minute without a lot of prep."

"She's older than Krystal," Adam said.

"Yes," Damon admitted. "Lane brings a different level of maturity to Calliope."

Adam straightened. "She's accepted the role."

It wasn't a question. The tension lacing each of his words surprised Megan. She loved Lane Gregory, way more than Krystal Kohl. Lane had the reputation of being nice and down-to-earth. Maybe those qualities weren't what Adam wanted in his next movie-set fling.

The thought of him with the talented actress left a bitter taste in Megan's mouth. Lane was too sweet for a man like Adam. But what happened between the two actors was none of Megan's business. Neither was the discussion they were having now. She wiped the bar where condensation had dripped off the pitchers.

Damon nodded.

Tight lines bracketed Eva's mouth. "Krystal is tall and thin. Lane is short and curvy. We're going to have to rethink everything, including the dinner gown."

"You have until Tuesday," Damon said.

Eva's startled gaze darted from the director to Chas. "What?"

"We have no leeway in the schedule," the producer admitted. "Adam is committed to another project after this."

Adam nodded.

"The other talent has commitments, too." Damon flashed the designer a big smile. "No worries. You've done this before, Eva. And won awards."

"I have." Eva shot a pointed look at the two wardrobe people, who pulled out their cell phones and started texting furiously. "I will again. But it's either going to kill the costume department or they'll want to kill me."

"Don't they already?" Adam teased.

Chas and Damon smiled. The two wardrobe people pressed their lips together as if not to agree with the actor. Megan felt herself nodding and ducked behind the bar to grab some napkins before Eva saw her.

"Tell us what you need," Chas said to the designer. "It's yours."

"You don't have the budget for what I need," Eva said.

Megan stood.

Adam waved his empty glass at her. "Refill, please."

She grabbed the water pitcher with lemon slices floating on top. As she stood next to Adam refilling his glass, awareness hummed through her. All that bare skin and muscle was hard to ignore. She wanted to touch him and see if he was as strong as he looked.

No, she didn't.

The guy needed to put on a shirt. And pants. Long ones.

She tightened her grip on the pitcher's handle.

"There goes your weekend," Adam said to her. "Mine, too."

Megan stared at him, confused. His clear, warm green eyes weren't helping matters. He had to be wearing contacts. She realized he was still talking to her. "What?"

"There will be a mad dash to get costumes for Lane. That means extra fittings and alterations," he explained. "Some of my clothes will change, too, since they were designed to go with Krystal's."

"Oh." Not the most intelligent response, but that was the only thing that came to mind as she looked at him. Darn the man with his hard, hot body, killer smile and amazing eyes. "I didn't think I'd have a lot of free time until after filming ended."

If she was still here then…

That burst of reality helped her regain her focus. She checked everyone's glasses so Eva wouldn't think she was slacking off. Or worse, swooning. No one else needed more to drink.

"You won't have much time," Adam said. "But the experience you gain during the shoot will be worth it."

Megan didn't know why he was talking to her. He must be bored because the others were busy. Unless he'd taken a fall out on the water and whacked his head on his surfboard. That was the only other logical explanation for the attention he was giving her. "Do you want me to get you anything else?"

Wicked laughter lit his eyes. "I can think of a few things…"

Megan inhaled sharply. She opened her mouth to speak, but no words came out.

"Be careful with what you offer around here, Texas." Adam spoke with a low voice so others wouldn't overhear.

The nickname bristled again. She was happy to have escaped Larkville, but she didn't hate the town. Okay, maybe a part of her did. But she missed a few things—her nephew, Brady, the yummy chocolate milkshakes and greasy fries at Gracie May's Diner, her dad's horse Storm and, of course, Rob. Megan missed him the most.

"Someone will take you up on it," Adam continued.

What was going on? He'd made fun of her on the walk to the house. Now he was cautioning her. That made zero sense. Then again, maybe things in Hollywood weren't supposed to add up the way they did back home. "I'll be more careful."

And she would be. Especially around him.

Megan wasn't a flirt or fan girl. She didn't dream of being swept off her feet by the gorgeous movie star or some other good-looking guy for that matter. Her heart belonged to her best friend. Or would once Rob realized they belonged together. He hadn't expressed any romantic interest in her and hadn't appreciated when she'd expressed hers in him. But that was okay…for now.

Her dad always said good things came to those who waited. She'd learned patience at a young age. This would be no different.

Parlaying this temporary, unpaid position into a permanent, salaried one was her priority. Rob was in Austin trying to get his own career going. But true love knew no bounds. The distance would make him realize how much she meant to him. Once she gained experience, she would be more employable, could live in Austin and work on location. She had it all planned out.

"I was talking about refreshments," she clarified.

"I know, but not everybody is me."

He sounded genuine, as if he cared what happened to her. That was odd, but she had to admit nice. Maybe there was more to Adam Noble than a pretty face and great body. "I'll remember that."

A cell phone, lying on the table, rang. He picked it up, looked at the number on the display screen, then stood. "Excuse me."

As he walked down the stairs to the beach to take his call, Megan carried the pitcher back to the bar. She didn't look back at Adam, though she was tempted. He was the first person who seemed to care about her beyond what errand or task she could do for them. Unless he was being nice as a ploy to get her in the sack.

No. She didn't think that was Adam's angle. He wouldn't waste his time on her. Not with so many beautiful women wanting to hop into his bed.

That was why his friendliness surprised and unnerved her.

Megan preferred honesty to flash. That was how she'd been raised back at the ranch. She wished her dad could have known he had two other children. She had no doubt he would do the right thing by them, whether they wanted it or not.

But Hollywood wasn't like that. It was full of flashy people. Total strangers whose strange world she'd step into. And that begged a question. Of all the people she'd met since arriving in Los Angeles, why was Adam Noble the one being so nice to her?

Adam stood on the sand in front of Chas's villa with his back to the water. He was far enough from the patio so no one would overhear his conversation with his agent, Sam Tomlinson, who once again showed impeccable timing with his phone call. "Lane Gregory is the new Calliope."

"She must have sweet-talked her fiancé into getting her the role," Sam said.

Lane's fiancé was Hugh Wilstead, the wealthy and powerful studio head backing the film. This movie was supposed to be a game changer for Adam. Instead of his typical action-adventure film, this new film was a serious drama piece. Not quite an indie production, which would have increased his award chances, but close enough to get him recognized for his acting ability. "Damon thinks she'll be good in the part."

"Definitely. But I'm more concerned what's going to happen when the cameras aren't rolling."

Lane's acting talent would help Adam in his pursuit of an award nomination. But she was also a costar man-eater, who would aggressively try to sleep with him in spite of her fiancé. "I'm not going to be her next boy toy."

"If Hugh finds out anything went on between the two of you outside of shooting…"

"I know." Rhys Rogers, Lane's costar in *The Island's Eye,* saw his burgeoning career come to a screeching halt after a fling with the lovely actress. She hadn't been engaged to Hugh then, only dating. "Rhys can't get hired for a reality TV gig now."

"Stay away from her," Sam cautioned.

"Hard to do when she'll be playing my wife." Some actors had no trouble figuring out where a role ended and reality began during shooting, but Adam sometimes did, especially if he felt a spark or connection with a costar. "Unless the script has a major rewrite this weekend, there are love scenes."

"Love scenes are fine as long as you're not rehearsing in private," Sam said. "Might be a good time to give celibacy a try."

"No reason to go crazy. I'll tell Lane the truth. I don't go out with engaged or married women."

"She may not be swayed so easily."

"She won't have a choice when I find someone else to help me relax during shooting."

"Please not another actress on the set," Sam said. "Catfights will be counterproductive."

Adam remembered the last time two actresses had gotten into it over him outside the Château Marmont. It had been flattering, but a mistake on his part. The publicity and negative vibe on the set easily could have been avoided if he hadn't been on such an ego trip back then. He enjoyed female companionship and seduction, but he had to be smart about it or he became nothing more than tabloid fodder. No one would take him seriously then. "I'll find a woman not on the cast list."

He noticed movement on the patio. He caught a glimpse of a pile of curly dark hair. Megan, the intern from Texas. That explained her slight twang.

A smile tugged on his lips. At least one good thing would come out of the casting change. Her internship would continue for at least another week. Eva would be too busy getting new costumes ready to fire Megan.

The thought of her sticking around longer made him happy. That was a little bizarre given she was a total stranger. But something about her appealed to him. Her eyes, yes, but he couldn't quite put his finger on what else it might be. Maybe her apparent dislike of him.

He looked up on the patio again, but didn't see her. No doubt she'd been ordered to do something else for someone.

Megan should make the most of her internship and time in Hollywood. She might have received a reprieve from being sent home in the next day or two, but she wouldn't last. Her quiet personality and self-conscious demeanor weren't cut out for Hollywood, but Adam hoped she would be here long enough to figure that out herself.

It was better for a person to change their dreams than have them stripped away. That had happened to his mother. His father had broken her heart when he took off. Since then, Adam had watched her chase pipe dreams and men. Nothing mattered to her except grabbing the golden ring—another wedding band. She would give up everything, including him, to find her one true love. Adam didn't want a broken dream to have that same kind of effect on anyone else, especially someone so quiet and shy, like Megan Calhoun.

CHAPTER THREE

THREE days later, Megan opened the hatchback of her car. Shoes and shoeboxes were strewn everywhere. She swallowed the sigh threatening to escape. She'd been sighing too much the past few days.

Besides, she had only herself to blame for this latest mess. She'd put down the backseats to give her more room to transport items. That hadn't worked out so well with the shoeboxes.

Megan tucked the car keys in the front pocket of her jeans.

She must have taken a few curves too fast. Not surprising, she'd been running late. Again. Driving was where she could make up time, if, and it was a big if, there wasn't any traffic on the road.

But standing here staring at all the sandals, pumps, flats and boots wasn't getting it done. She needed to put the shoes back into their boxes and carry them inside before Lane Gregory's fitting. That was the reason Megan had been given strict instructions with an impossible time frame.

Eva must want her to fail. Megan matched up boxes with lids. That was the only explanation for being stuck in interning purgatory. A headache threatened to erupt.

She rubbed her temples. It didn't help. More caffeine might. That stuff had been keeping her going the past two days. What she needed was a sit-down meal with fresh vegetables and a decent night's sleep. Neither looked likely in the near future.

Megan arranged the boxes so she could see what was missing what. Gathering the pieces for today's costume fittings had meant killer hours, irregular meal times and little, if any, sleep. Not just for her, but everyone working wardrobe and costumes on the film.

Talk about an insane schedule.

But she couldn't give up. That wasn't the Calhoun way. Her dad might not physically be here any longer, but his spirit and memory lived on. She wanted him to be proud of her.

She picked up a shoebox with a single silver slingback sandal inside. The matching shoe had to be here somewhere.

As she sorted through the shoes, putting them into the correct boxes, she imagined what awful task they—okay, Eva—would assign next. A long list of horrible, degrading tasks ran through Megan's mind. She half laughed.

Hard to believe she was working so hard for free.

Not only working, but driving.

She'd put a couple hundred miles on her car running errands around town for Eva and company. Granted Megan would be reimbursed for mileage and gas, but hazard pay for being forced to drive on the L.A. freeways should be included.

Something silver near the left passenger door caught Megan's eye. The sandal. She grabbed hold of it. Her cell phone vibrated in her back jeans pocket.

Unbelievable. She grimaced. As soon as she was close to finishing an errand, a text would arrive telling her what to do next. It was as if a camera followed her every move so she would never have a spare moment. Coincidence, yes. She didn't think Hollywood was that wired, but it was still weird.

She removed her phone from her pocket, but hesitated looking at the display screen.

Please don't make me go back to the warehouse clear across town. The one I just came from.

That had happened twice yesterday during bumper-to-bumper traffic on the 405. She'd had to drive from Santa Monica to Van Nuys and back again.

Talk about a total nightmare. She shivered.

But if asked to make that drive again, Megan would. She would smile and drive wherever they asked. She would do whatever it took in the hopes of gaining real costume design experience with this internship.

However unlikely that looked at the moment.

She placed the shoe in the box with its match, put the lid on top, then read the name on the cell phone's display screen.

Rob.

Finally.

Usually a thrill shot through her each time she heard from him, but today she felt a sliver of annoyance. She'd been sending him texts all week, but he hadn't replied to any of them. No doubt he'd been as busy getting settled in Austin and starting his new job as she was here in Los Angeles. But she didn't see why he couldn't take two minutes out of his day—thirty seconds even—to text her back.

Megan read his message.

How's showbiz?

She thought about everything she'd been doing, from driving all over L.A. to meeting Adam Noble. The guy, or at least images of him wearing only a pair of shorts with water dripping down his tanned skin, had taken up permanent residency in her thoughts. She chalked it up to him being nice to her. But she'd much rather think about someone else.

Someone like Rob.

Her perfect guy. Even if he wasn't the best at keeping in touch with her.

She typed a one-word reply summing up her first week in town.

Exhausting.

Everything about her internship tired her out. But in spite of the exhaustion, she honestly couldn't think of anywhere else she'd rather be than here in Hollywood. Well, except Austin with Rob.

"So you can smile."

The familiar male voice startled her. She glanced up from her phone display to see Adam Noble standing next to her. He wore a pair of khaki cargo shorts with a button-down, light blue, short-sleeved shirt and hi-tech-looking sports sandals. His brown hair was casually yet artfully tousled. His easy smile showed a gleaming row of straight, white teeth. He looked…good.

Not that she cared how he looked outside of him wearing one of the costumes. She slid her cell phone into the back pocket of her jeans. "Everyone can smile, Mr. Noble."

"Adam."

Oh, yeah. He'd told her to call him by his first name. She stared at the shoes scattered in her car. She needed to get busy.

"You didn't smile at Chas's place," Adam said.

She put a pair of black ankle boots into a large shoebox. "I was working."

"You're working now."

"Trying to work," she mumbled.

Her cell phone beeped. Rob. Anticipation at his quick response to her last text surged—the way it did on the day her copy of *Vogue* arrived in the mail. Maybe absence *was* making his heart grow fonder. Megan fought the urge to whip out her phone, but that would be rude with Adam here. She didn't want to get in trouble for texting when she should be delivering the shoes. Not that Adam would tattle. Or maybe he would…

Not worth the risk. She matched another pair of shoes.

"I know why you're smiling."

Adam's playful tone drew her attention away from the shoes and on to him. "Why?"

His green eyes twinkled with mischief. "I saw you with your phone. Your boyfriend is texting you."

In her dreams.

Okay, Rob was a boy. He was also her friend. But he wasn't

her boyfriend. Not yet, anyway. Sometimes—a lot of times lately—he frustrated her. But she hoped once he realized how good they would be as a couple everything would fall into place.

Still, who she exchanged texts with was no one's business, especially Adam's. "I'm sorry, but I need to get these shoes sorted and inside before the fittings begin."

"You're discreet."

His charming smile sent her pulse skittering. She chalked up the reaction to tiredness.

"I like that," he added.

His compliment made her straighten. She wasn't used to being complimented. Most people in Larkville had pegged her as an oddity years ago. Being friends with Rob, who might be a geek but was also the mayor's grandson, was the only thing that kept her from being an outcast.

Megan reached for another pair of shoes. Her hand trembled. Uh-oh. She couldn't let herself be affected by Adam. The guy was an actor, a player who had more lines than a pad of graph paper. The realization irritated her. "I don't have time to talk right now. I'm running late."

"You have a mess on your hands."

Captain Obvious seemed as fitting a name for him as Adam. She searched for a red leather pump. It had to be here somewhere. "Yes."

"I'll help."

"That's not…"

Her cell phone vibrated again. Rob.

Adam held up the missing red shoe. "Where does this go?"

Okay, maybe she could use the help. The sooner she finished this task, the sooner she could get back to Rob. "In the brown box."

Adam helped her sort the rest of the shoes. Having his assistance made the task go faster. She put on the lids, then stacked the boxes. "Thanks so much. I won't have time to grab lunch, but I won't be in too much trouble for being late."

"You haven't eaten?"

The concern in Adam's voice surprised her.

"I've eaten. Well, not today. I've been living off pizza, fast food and coffee. I was hoping to have a sit-down meal. Maybe tomorrow." Megan picked up five boxes. The different sizes made balancing difficult, but she managed. "I'd better get these inside."

Boxes slipped.

Adam straightened the stack with one hand while his other rested on the small of her back. "Be careful."

No kidding. The jersey knit fabric of her T-shirt kept their skin from touching, but awareness seeped through her. Heat, too.

The imprint of his large, warm hand left her tongue-tied. She took two steps back. "Th-thanks. I've got them."

"You have a lot of boxes," he said. "I'll carry some in."

Megan's brow knotted. "But you're the star…"

"I was trying to get a rise out of you by saying that."

"It worked."

"And now you're not going to let me forget I said that."

"You are the star."

He shook his head, but looked amused.

"Don't worry," she said. "I won't be able to remind you about it too much. I doubt our paths will cross much after filming begins."

"They call it shooting, not filming."

"I didn't know that. Thanks."

Not seeing Adam would be kind of a bummer. He was the only person who had not only been nice but also offered to help her. That made Adam Noble the closest thing to a friend she had in Los Angeles. Not that she had anything in common with him.

His eyes darkened. "I was a jerk to you at Chas's place."

Megan drew back, careful not to let any of the boxes fall. She never would have expected Adam to own up to his behavior. She wasn't sure what to make of it. Him. *Hollywood*

A-lister and *all-around nice guy* seemed to be contradictory terms, yet he appeared to be both. "I'm figuring out that's how things work here when you're new."

"That's not how things should work." Adam picked up several of the shoeboxes, enough to save her two trips. "Let me make it up to you."

Once again, Adam had done—make that said—the unexpected. His display of chivalry confused her. He seemed so different from everyone else she'd met this week. She wanted to know how he thought things should work in Hollywood, but he didn't need to make anything up to her. Not really. "You are, by helping me."

"This is nothing," Adam said. "Let me buy you lunch after the fitting. We can have a sit-down meal in the commissary. No eating on the run or in your car."

She hadn't known what he'd meant by making it up to her, but a lunch invite hadn't been it. A part of Megan wanted to accept. She could use some company and conversation. Both were sparse around here. Not to mention she was hungry. But his reputation as a ladies' man made her wonder if he had an ulterior motive. Maybe he was the type of man who always wanted women to like him. "You don't have to do that."

"I want to."

"I might not finish at the same time as you."

"I'm not in a hurry."

"I might be sent on another errand."

"You might not."

His attention flattered her. Until Megan remembered how he'd focused on each person at the table in Malibu. Maybe Adam was the kind of person who didn't like to feel under obligation.

"What do you say?" he asked. "Give me your number and I'll text you when I'm finished."

If Adam felt he owed her, her accepting his invitation would make things square between them. If he had asked her out for more nefarious reasons, she could handle it. Him. Nate had taught her a few self-defense moves he'd learned in his military training. But she honestly didn't think she had to worry about that with Adam.

Truth was, having lunch with him appealed to Megan. Eating her meals on the go and alone was getting old fast. She was figuring out the people you knew in the business were as important as what you knew. Being on good terms with a movie star of Adam Noble's stature couldn't hurt her, especially when it came to finding a permanent position. She would need people to give her recommendations. His name would carry weight.

"Sure," she said. "I'd like that."

Two hours later, Adam stood in one of the dressing rooms in the wardrobe department. People, mainly women, scurried in and out, buzzing around him like bees as they scribbled notes.

He was nothing more than a living, breathing mannequin. Clothes came off. Others went on. His white boxer briefs were the only item that remained on his body the entire time.

A mix of perfumes wafted in the air. Adam recognized the scent of one, Chanel No. 5. His mother wore that.

He preferred the way Megan smelled—like springtime. Light, sunny, a little flowery. Not a chemical scent manufactured in a lab, but the real deal.

He was looking forward to having lunch with her. She was different from the people he normally came in contact with, so unaffected.

She'd disappeared after they'd brought in the shoes. He kept hoping she'd breeze into his dressing room.

The costumer, a woman in her early thirties named Kenna, straightened the shoulders of his tuxedo jacket. "I'd forgotten how well this tuxedo fits you. Forty-two long, right?"

Adam nodded. He'd worked with her before on the Roman gods epic blockbuster that had made him a bankable star. Her hair had been blond then, not a flaming red. The new color suited Kenna as did the vintage clothing she always wore. "Thanks to you."

With a grin, she adjusted his sleeves. "I wish all actors had wide shoulders like yours. Suits and tuxedos look so much nicer."

Adam would wear the tux during the first turning point when his character, Maxwell Caldecott, became the scapegoat for his wealthy father-in-law's illegal activity and was arrested. But the tux made him think of something other than that pivotal scene—award season. He was banking on this drama, a character piece with big emotions, to catapult him into an award nominee and winner.

He winked. "I bet you say that to all the actors."

The set costumer, a woman in her late twenties named Rosie, tied his bow tie. "Only the hot ones."

"The truth comes out," he teased.

The women smiled at him. These weren't flirtatious come-ons, but genuine grins.

Adam appreciated their good humor. He couldn't imagine the past few days had been easy on them. They both had the same dark circles under their eyes as Megan. He wondered what she was doing right now.

"Turn," Rosie said.

He did.

"Now for the accessories." Kenna glanced at her clipboard. "We've changed a couple of things so they wouldn't clash with Lane's costumes. She's not a big fan of gold."

Rosie glanced in a marked container. "Speaking of which, where is the new wedding band?"

"Eva had it earlier," Kenna said.

Rosie sent a text. "We'll have it in a minute. Once we get Eva's approval on this ensemble, you can go."

Kenna nodded. "We'll tag the items, then it's time for a much needed lunch break."

Her words made him think about Megan again. He thought she would say no to his invitation, but he was pleased she hadn't. Buying her lunch would make up for the way he'd teased her at Chas's house.

As if on cue, Megan entered the dressing area with a small ring box in her hands. She didn't look at him.

All business. Adam's grin widened. Well, except for her casual clothes. She'd removed her jacket. She was wearing the same baggy pink T-shirt and jeans she'd worn at the beach. Her wild, curly brown hair was piled and clipped on top of her head once again. But the earrings were new. She hadn't worn jewelry before. Add a pair of smart-girl glasses and she really would have the geek-chic look down. Her cheeks were flushed pink, as if she were exercising. Most likely running errands.

"You have Maxwell's ring?" Kenna asked.

Megan nodded. "Eva said there are extra cuff links if you need them."

Kenna glanced at the clipboard. "We're using the silver ones with the diamond chips."

Adam noticed Megan seemed more comfortable here than at the beach house and less agitated than at her car earlier. Not only her demeanor, but her posture and voice. Except for the way she was dressed, she fit right in.

"Show Adam the ring," Kenna instructed.

Megan shuffled forward, her feet encased in white canvas sneakers. She looked a little pale, more tired than when he'd seen her earlier. No doubt hungry, too.

"Our paths cross again, Texas," Adam said.

Lines creased Rosie's forehead. Her gaze bounced between them. "You two know each other?"

"We met at Chas's house a few days ago," Adam explained.

Gossip spread like wildfire on sets. He watched what he said around the crew. Not that anything was going on with the intern. Or any other woman at the moment. Unfortunately.

"I had to take Eva the right portfolio," Megan explained.

Rosie sighed. "The day our lives ended."

Kenna nodded.

Megan removed a platinum-and-diamond ring from the box. Light reflected off the row of diamonds, sending colorful prisms dancing on the walls and ceiling.

Whoa. Adam wouldn't wear that kind of ring in real life, but he could see his character Maxwell wanting something flashy like that. "That's fancier than the original gold band I was going to wear."

"Lane picked it out," Kenna explained. "She felt since she's playing the role of your wife, she should decide what kind of wedding band Maxwell wears."

"So Maxwell is into bling now," Adam teased.

"He will be once you're wearing it," Kenna said. "Put it on his left ring finger, Texas."

Megan's eyes widened at the nickname, and not in a good way. Oops.

He expected her to say something to Kenna, but Megan didn't. Damn. She couldn't. Not as an intern. She didn't dare risk stepping on toes around here.

One more strike against him. More to make up to her. Adam would force her to order dessert. Something chocolate. Most women, even chronic dieters, loved chocolate.

Megan held the ring between her index and thumb. "Left hand, please."

Her serious expression, coupled with her slight Texas twang, made Adam bite back a laugh. She was trying so hard to be professional when it looked like what she really needed was a decent meal, a big hug and a comfy pillow to rest her head. He'd offered the first. He wouldn't mind providing all three.

Adam extended his arm and flexed his fingers to make it easier on her.

As she reached toward him with the ring, her hand trembled ever so slightly.

Her nervousness tugged at Adam's heart. So sweet, the quintessential girl-next-door. He'd bet she wasn't from a big town in Texas. She had small town written all over her both in her dress and mannerisms. Hollywood and Firebreather could eat her alive. He hoped that didn't happen.

The cool metal of the ring touched his fingertip. A slight shock jolted him. Must be static from the carpet.

Megan slid the ring the rest of the way onto his finger. Her skin, soft and warm, brushed his. She tensed, pressing her lips together.

He wanted to lighten the mood and see her smile again. Having her breathe wouldn't be a bad idea, either. She wasn't the type to be easily charmed. He'd tried only to crash and burn. Humor might work. "Do you know how many women would love to trade places with you right now?"

Those beautiful brown eyes of hers mesmerized him with their intensity. Something flickered in them, flashed. "Oh, I don't know. A star of your caliber? I suppose…millions."

Her lighthearted tone matched the mischievous smile gracing her lips.

Objective achieved. He liked her sense of humor. Adam grinned. "At least that many."

Kenna laughed. "But none of us."

Rosie nodded. "Not unless we want to face Firebreather's wrath."

That familiar V formed above the bridge of Megan's nose. "We're not allowed to be fans?"

"Oh, we can be fans. Just not a certain kind of fan," Kenna explained with a pointed look.

"That's a big no-no," Rosie added.

Megan looked genuinely confused. "I have no idea what you're talking about."

As far as Adam knew, there weren't any firm rules about relationships on film sets as long as they didn't interfere with the production schedule. He'd had his fair share of them. His only requirement was when the shoot ended so did the fling. "What's a big no-no?"

"Set romances happen all the time, but Eva won't allow us to get involved with the lead actors," Kenna said.

Adam flinched. He was a lead actor. "Seriously?"

Kenna nodded. "Eva thinks the entire crew should keep their distance from the talent, but she has no say over what they do."

"Nothing personal, Adam." Kenna stuck her pencil behind

her ear. "But some actors wouldn't hesitate to have a crew member fired if they didn't want a person around any longer. That's why Eva tells us to stay away from the leads. It isn't worth losing our jobs over, and it's too big a pain for her to replace us."

Megan exhaled on a sigh. "That makes sense."

Maybe to her, but not to him. Adam was offended lead actors had such a bad rep with crew members. Not that he'd ever gotten involved with one, but there was always a first time.

His gaze rested on Megan, who wasn't his type and likely had a boyfriend, the person she'd been texting.

But, on second thought, when had he ever let minor details like that stop him?

Never.

In the costume workroom, Megan sorted through the scarves that hadn't made the final cut during Lane Gregory's fitting. Megan tried to focus on the task at hand, but all she could think about was Adam.

What was he doing? His costume fitting had ended twenty minutes ago, but he hadn't texted her about lunch.

Thinking about him sent her pulse skittering. He had looked so gorgeous in that tux. Suave and debonair. A perfect leading man, yes. But he'd also reminded her of a...

Groom.

Megan swallowed.

When she'd approached him with the ring, she'd thought he looked a lot like a husband-to-be waiting for his bride at the altar.

A silly thought. No doubt due to sleep deprivation and lack of healthy food.

But when she'd slid the wedding ring onto his finger she'd felt a slight shock, a prick of static electricity. Thank goodness the ring had been over his finger or she would have dropped it.

But she hadn't. She'd held on to the ring and done her job. End of story.

No reason to turn this into something it wasn't. She was tired. Nothing else would explain why, for a moment in the dressing room, she'd forgotten everything and everyone.

Kenna, Rosie, even Rob.

Rob.

Megan's stomach dropped to her feet. How could she forget her best friend? Her future boyfriend and husband? She'd never checked his text message after bringing in the shoeboxes with Adam.

Guilt coated her mouth. She'd been distracted. That was all. As soon as she finished with the scarves, she would not only reply but also give Rob a quick call, if only to leave a voice mail.

That was if Adam didn't text her in the meanwhile.

She reached for a lime-green scarf. Her fingertips brushed across the soft fabric. Cashmere. But not even the luxurious fabric made her feel better.

Agreeing to have lunch with Adam had been a big mistake. Especially after hearing Kenna and Rosie's warning about Eva wanting them to stay away from lead actors.

Okay, eating lunch with Adam wasn't a date. He was simply paying her back, righting a wrong, evening the score. But after seeing how hot he looked in that tux and how she kept thinking about him, spending any time with him seemed like a really bad idea. She couldn't afford to mess up this internship. Nor was there room in her life—her heart—for a crush on a movie star.

Megan glanced at her watch. Two o'clock.

Maybe he'd changed his mind or forgotten about lunch.

She ignored a prick of disappointment. Not getting together with him would be for the best.

Footsteps sounded in the hall.

Adam.

Anticipation made her glance toward the doorway.

A short woman with spiky bleached-blond hair and a tight black miniskirt and purple blouse hurried past.

Megan exhaled the breath she'd been holding. She put away the scarves.

Whether Adam blew her off or not, she needed to focus on the positive—the costume fitting. She was still running errands and delivering items to people here at the lot, but she hadn't been asked to get anyone food to eat or a beverage to drink. This was the longest time she'd spent in the department since arriving on Monday. Maybe things were changing. A satisfied smile settled on her lips.

"Ready for lunch?"

Megan dropped two scarves onto the floor. She glanced over her shoulder.

Adam leaned casually against the door frame, making her wonder how long he'd been standing there. His shoulders looked wider than normal, even though he no longer wore the tux, but the same T-shirt and shorts she'd seen him wearing earlier.

Darn the man. He looked just as hot dressed casually. She cleared her dry throat. "I thought you were going to text me."

"I decided to come by instead."

"I need to put the scarves away."

"I'm in no rush, Tex."

She sighed. "Please don't call me that."

He grinned. "It's cute."

Her heart did a little two-step. "It's not my name."

"No, but it's memorable."

That was the problem. The name reminded her of Larkville, the place she wanted to forget. Sure, she loved her family, the way you were supposed to love your brothers and sister, but they were so wrapped up in their own lives they didn't need her. They never had.

A weight pressed down on the center of Megan's chest. "This might take a while. Go to lunch without me."

"I can't imagine seven scarves taking that long to put away."

Were there only seven? She made a quick count. Seven. Guess it was too late to hope Eva would appear and demand

Megan run another errand or do some other task. "I've been thinking…"

"That can be dangerous."

Especially when it came to him. She mustered her courage. "I thought about what Kenna and Rosie said during your fitting."

"About lead actors and the crew."

Megan nodded. "Us having lunch probably isn't a good idea."

"I invited you out to eat, not to have sex in my trailer." Desire flared in his eyes and made her mouth go dry. "Though if you'd rather pay a visit there…"

Heat burned her cheeks. She tried to think of a witty response. Tried and failed. All she could think about was his trailer and what might happen during a visit. Her entire face must be as red as the cherry preserves her mom and sister, Jess, used to can.

Laughter danced in Adam's eyes. "No trailer today. Just the cafeteria for an innocent lunch."

He emphasized the last two words, but Megan doubted he knew the definition of *innocent.* The guy was wickedly charming. Regular guys—the kind who didn't star in movies and ooze sex appeal 24/7—rarely gave her the time of day. Granted, she never encouraged male attention because the only man she spent time with was Rob, who didn't notice any of her encouragements. But she couldn't understand why Adam was acting this way. He could do much better than her.

"You have to be hungry," he added.

Her shrug gave way to a nod. She was starving. As if on cue, her stomach growled.

He stepped closer and held her hand.

Warmth seeped through her fingers and hand and up her arm. His skin felt rough, calloused like her father's and brothers' hands. But there was nothing familiar about the heat rushing up her arm and the way her pulse accelerated like a thoroughbred out of the starting gate. The urge to bolt for the nearest exit was strong.

Adam gave a gentle tug. "It's just lunch. No big deal."

Maybe not to him. Megan wasn't so sure. She liked Adam holding her hand. Liked it a lot. And that was oh-so-wrong. On many levels. A funny tingling sensation settled in the pit of her stomach.

Pulling her hand away and giving him some excuse why she couldn't have lunch today was the smart thing to do. That was what she should do.

He squeezed her hand. "Come on. Let's go."

CHAPTER FOUR

So MUCH for doing the smart thing.

Sitting across from Adam at a table in the studio's cafeteria, Megan's nerves threatened to get the best of her. Her foot tapped uncontrollably. She pressed her toe against the tile floor. It didn't ease her jitters.

Megan knew better. She should have never agreed to lunch. But when he squeezed her hand in the workroom, she'd caved like a house of cards built on a wobbly teeter-totter. Resolve and common sense had disappeared faster than the hush puppies served at Nan's Bunk'n'Grill out on I-38.

Done in by a pretty face, warm skin and tingles.

Pathetic.

Except the tingles were out of this world. She'd never felt anything like them.

The din of customers' conversations rose above the instrumental music playing from hidden speakers. Using her fork, she pushed around the baby greens, Gorgonzola, pears and candied walnuts. She didn't know why she'd ordered a salad in addition to a sandwich, fries and dessert.

Adam's plate contained a roast beef sandwich and steamed veggies. "So what do you think of the place?" he asked.

As she ate a forkful of baby greens, she surveyed the cafeteria. It was more like a café with modern decor and not one pastel-colored tray in sight. People filled the tables, whether for a late lunch or midafternoon snack she couldn't tell. Coffee mugs and water glasses seemed to be in a race for the drink of choice. No doubt the low calories appealed to the masses.

"This is nothing like we have back home where greasy fries and hash browns reign supreme. Gracie May calls them Texas Taters. Not to be confused with the ever popular Texas Toast." The knot in Megan's stomach tightened. "I'm rambling, aren't I?"

Adam wiped his mouth with a napkin. "No, I like hearing you talk."

He would be the first. Well, next to Rob and her dad.

"Thanks. But being at a film studio is a little surreal." Megan lowered her voice. "I recognize a few people. Actors I've seen on TV and in the movies."

Adam smiled at her. "You'll get used to it."

"I don't know about that." She pushed her salad plate to the side and scooted the plate with a Reuben sandwich and French fries in front of her. "I keep wanting to pinch myself to make sure I'm really here, in Hollywood, and not dreaming. Though they're not always good dreams. I sometimes feel like I'm sitting on a chair covered with thumbtacks pointy side up."

"Ouch." He raised his water glass. "You need to relax. Loosen up."

"I don't think that's possible." At least not when he was with her. Something about Adam Noble put Megan on edge, made her nerve endings stand at attention and her senses shift into overdrive. She toyed with the napkin on her lap. It ripped in half. She needed to calm down. "Was today a typical fitting?"

"Fairly typical. More rushed due to Lane joining the cast so late. But last-minute changes are nothing new. Cast. Crew. Costumes. Script." Adam took a sip of water. "How did you like the fitting?"

She leaned forward with excitement. "It was so awesome."

"That's a strong adjective."

With a shrug, she sat back. "You wouldn't understand."

He raised a piece of broccoli with his fork. "Try me."

Rob supported her interest in fashion, but he had zero interest in talking about clothing. Adam sounded interested. But for all she knew he was being polite. "Really?"

"Yes."

Not saying anything would be rude. He had invited her to lunch. What's the worst that could happen? She'd been teased and taunted her entire life. Adam might tease, but his ribbing could never cut her down like the people back home.

Truth was, she was bursting at the seams to talk to someone about her internship. She'd been going over things in her head, but that wasn't much fun or helpful. If Adam wanted to listen she was more than willing to spill. "Well, up until today's fitting I've spent my time driving all over Los Angeles and doing the jobs no one else wants to do."

"The life of an intern."

"I get that's what I'm supposed to be doing," she admitted. "But during the fitting I finally saw what working with costumes was like. I was allowed to help, too."

He set his fork on this plate. "That would be pretty awesome."

She nodded. "It was eye-opening and showed me how much I have to learn."

"What do you mean?"

"I dressed characters in theater throughout college. I thought I had a good eye when it came to clothes, but today when the costumers and dressers pointed out things that need to be fixed or changed I realized how much I'd missed."

"They pay attention to minute details."

"I know," she said. "I felt like I was watching an episode of *What Not to Wear,* except the show was on steroids with a warehouse-size closet of clothing and accessories to choose from. Then each piece was put under a fashion microscope. A little overwhelming, but I learned a lot listening to Lane talk about how Calliope would dress."

"Some actors like to involve themselves in the costume process."

"Lane sure does. Do you?"

"Yeah. I usually have a good idea about what my characters would wear. Think about what's in your closet. A lot of pieces have stories behind them. A character's wardrobe is no different."

Wow. Megan had no idea a guy would see clothing that way. At least not a straight one. She was impressed. "I didn't think it would be so much of a collaboration. I thought it would be more one-sided with the costume designer deciding everything."

Someone waved at Adam. He acknowledged them with a nod. "It's give and take between actor and costume designer. The camera people can also get involved if they have lighting or color concerns."

"Was the tux one of your suggestions?" she asked.

"The scene called for formal wear. Eva and I agreed on the designer because of Maxwell's background and need to fit in with his wealthy in-laws. But when push comes to shove Eva has final say. Though she's pretty good about letting the talent think we're in control."

Megan remembered something Eva had said to Lane. "Aha."

"You saw it in action today."

"Yes, but I don't think Lane realized that's what Eva was doing."

"I'm sure she didn't." Adam waved to someone calling his name. He seemed to know everyone. "One thing I have to say about Eva. She understands actors as well as she does costumes."

"The woman is meticulous." Changes were made to a costume—color, accessories or something new altogether—until Eva deemed the outfit acceptable. Then photographs would be taken, items tagged and stored. "I can't wait to see how it looks on film."

"Sometimes directors show dailies on Fridays. Keeps morale high among the crew. Damon's pretty good about doing stuff like that."

Megan dipped a French fry in ketchup. "I can't believe filming, I mean, the shoot starts in a couple of days."

"No reason to be nervous."

She stared down her nose at him. "What makes you think I'm nervous?"

"I was my first time on a film set," he admitted. "I am a little anxious with this shoot. I have high hopes for this film."

His openness made her feel less self-conscious. "Okay, I'm nervous. Though I'm sure I'll spend all my time running errands and won't be able to see any of the shoot."

"They might need your help on call days with lots of background artists."

Kenna had told Megan that extras on movie sets were often called background artists. "I hope so. I need some real experience if I'm going to find a permanent job out here once my internship is finished."

His gaze narrowed. "You want to stay in L.A."

"Yes." She didn't plan on returning to Larkville until October for her father's memorial celebration at the Fall Festival. Even then she would only stay for the weekend. "It's the best place to build up my résumé. It's rather light at the moment."

"Your family…"

Her chest tightened. "My sister, Jess, her five-year-old son, Brady, and my brother Holt still live in Larkville. My other brother Nate is in the army. But cattle and ranching aren't my things. I don't really fit in. The town caters to livestock and cowboys, not the arts and fashion. I have different interests and felt stifled creatively. Even the way I dressed made people uncomfortable."

Adam's brows slanted. "Jeans, T-shirts and sneakers made people uncomfortable?"

"This was before I, um, started dressing like this." She shifted positions in her chair. "Anyway, people thought…they still think I'm…different."

"Nothing wrong with being different."

That was what Rob always told her. Easy for him to say since everyone liked and accepted him. "True. But when you're a Calhoun people in Larkville have certain expectations, especially about fitting in."

Including other Calhouns. Her appetite disappeared.

Adam stared at her. "That's gotta be hard."

He had no idea. But no sense dwelling on things she couldn't change. "That's one reason I didn't go back after I graduated college. If everything works out like I've planned, I'll be here for a while."

"You've got plans."

Big ones. She nodded.

"A planner?"

She raised her chin. "Yes."

Amusement gleamed in his eyes. "I wasn't slamming you. Just asking a question."

"Sorry, I'm a little defensive about a few things."

"People back home didn't like your plans, either."

"You'll never amount to anything if you pursue costume design. Forget about working in the film industry. You'll never cut it. You won't be able to support yourself, either. And I'm not about to give you money to live on while you chase some ridiculous dream."

Her late mother's words echoed through Megan's head. She stabbed her fork into a slice of pear. "No, but that hasn't stopped me."

"Perseverance is the key to success."

"I've heard it's all about having the right connections."

"That's a part of it, too, but if you give up it doesn't matter who you know." He picked up his sandwich. "How's your plan working out so far?"

"Too early to tell."

"Cautious. I like that."

"I've learned being too cocky about the potential success of a plan can lead to big disappointment."

"Sounds like there's a story there."

"I tried to run away from home," Megan admitted. "I had it all planned out, but I didn't count on one thing."

"Common sense kicking in," he joked.

"I was fourteen."

"That explains it," he said. "So what didn't you count on?"

"My best friend, Rob. I told him my plans. He wouldn't let me go on my own. Told me he was coming with me."

"Sounds like a good guy."

"A great guy and also the mayor's grandson." Thinking about Rob made her feel all warm and cozy, the exact opposite to how she felt around Adam. "We got as far as the bus station, then the chief of police showed up."

"That's a plan-buster."

"No kidding." Only now could she laugh at the horrified expressions on her family's faces. Her mother had been mortified that Megan had dragged a fine, upstanding young man like Rob into her teenage rebellion. "I was *so* grounded after that. My parents took away my sewing machine. I was devastated. But I'm much better at planning things now."

He grinned. "And who you tell about those plans."

She smiled. "Exactly."

"Remember, you can't plan everything," Adam said. "Some of the best moments in life just happen."

"For some people, yes. But I'm not really into spontaneity and surprises." That was one reason she was relieved to be in California, not home having to deal with two unexpected half siblings. Her half sister, Ellie Patterson, was now living in Larkville and dating the town's sheriff, Jed Jackson. "I like to know what's coming."

"Not knowing what's around the corner is half the fun."

Megan shrugged. "I still have fun."

"I hope so." Adam winked. "All work and no play makes Megan…"

"And Adam," she joined in.

"A dull girl."

"Boy," she said at the same time.

He smiled at her.

She smiled back.

Something seemed to pass between them, as if an invisible cord suddenly connected them. A ball of heat ignited in her stomach.

What was going on? Okay, he was gorgeous. Nice. And...

Time to chill. She took a sip of her lemonade to cool her down. "Though I can't imagine you ever being a dull boy."

"I prefer excitement and keeping the adrenaline pumping to dullness."

"That's why you surf."

"And backcountry snowboard, skydive, bungee jump and BASE jump, too."

"An extreme-sport aficionado."

"Guilty as charged."

"Your family must worry about you."

As he stared into his water glass, his green eyes darkened. "It's just my mom and me. She's not that much of a worrier. At least not about what I'm doing."

Adam sounded resigned, not bitter. Good for him. Megan wasn't quite there yet. "Do you see your mom a lot?"

"No," he said. "She lives in Beverly Hills, but keeps herself busy. She enjoys traveling. She's on a cruise now."

"She must be proud of you."

"My mom likes having a famous movie star as a son." A touch of bitterness now crept into his tone. "It sure beats working two jobs and having to move to a new apartment every six months or so."

"That would be tough. For both of you."

He raised his water glass. "You learn how to make new friends fast."

"An important skill to have." One she didn't possess. Making friends was as hard for her as fitting in. She hadn't shared the same interests as other kids. Her dad had said she was a city girl stuck in a Podunk cow town. That had always angered her mom. But Megan appreciated how her dad understood her longing to get away. But she had to admit that so far she hadn't fit as easily into Hollywood as she thought she would, either. "I've lived in the same house my entire life except for four years of college and coming here."

"There's something to be said for that kind of familiarity."

Maybe if they'd moved around she would have found a place she fit in. But her dad's heart had always been in the land and the cattle. Hard to take those with him. "I suppose."

"Your parents must like Larkville or they would have moved away."

Her insides twisted at the reality of her new world.

"My parents are...dead." Saying that felt weird. Wrong. "I'm sorry to say it so bluntly. I'm still getting used to my dad being gone. He died in October. Pneumonia. My mom died of a heart attack three years ago."

Adam reached across the table and covered Megan's hand with his. "I'm so sorry."

His skin was warm, but rough. The touch was meant to comfort, but heat shot up her arm. She focused on his face. "My dad told me we're never given anything we can't handle. I keep reminding myself of that."

And if she wanted to handle her internship the right way, she'd better pull her hand away right now.

Megan did. She immediately missed Adam's warmth. But it was better this way. Safer.

"Are you close to your siblings?" Adam asked.

"No. But we never have been. Holt is thirty, Nate is twenty-eight and Jess is twenty-six. I've always been seen as more of a pest than an equal in their eyes even though I'm twenty-two now."

Megan ate another French fry.

As if that explained why none of them had showed up to her college graduation a couple of weeks ago. Jess had been too busy with her new husband. Holt was away dealing with a friend who was terminally ill. Nate hadn't even called to say he wasn't coming. Megan had no idea where he was, if her soldier brother was alive or dead. If not for Rob and his family she would have been on her own after the commencement service. Without her best friend, she wouldn't have anyone who cared about her.

"My dad was the one who'd kept the family together after Mom died. Now that he's gone, it's been…different." Megan might have three siblings and two half siblings, but she felt so alone, an orphan in every sense of the word. "But what am I going to do?"

"Move to Los Angeles and make a new life for yourself."

She appreciated that Adam understood. He was so easy to talk to. "My dad knew the ranch wasn't where I belonged. He wanted me to pursue my dreams. That's one reason I hope I succeed. To show him he was right about me."

And that her mom was wrong.

Three women sashayed down the aisle with swaying hips and expert hair-flipping skills, but Adam never looked in their direction even though they were supermodel gorgeous. Instead, he kept his attention focused solely on her. "I'm rooting for you."

"Thanks." One of the women glared at Megan. As if she were any kind of competition. Still she appreciated how Adam made her feel special when she was so obviously out of her league. "I have a feeling I'm going to need all the help I can get."

As they ate and talked about their favorite baseball teams and vacation spots, she realized Adam hadn't mentioned his father. "You said it was you and your mom. Your dad—"

"Was a total jerk," Adam interrupted. "He took off when I was a little kid. Haven't heard from him since. But I don't want to talk about that."

Megan didn't blame Adam. Her heart hurt for him and what he must have gone through as a kid. At least she'd had two parents when she was a kid, even if one hadn't liked her much. "What do you want to talk about?"

Adam pushed his plate away. Not a bit of his roast beef sandwich remained. Someone else had been hungry.

He leaned back in his chair. "You."

The way he looked at her sent her temperature inching upward. "I'm all we've been talking about."

"I want to know more."

"There isn't much more to tell." She lowered her voice. "In case you haven't figured it out, I'm boring."

His smile crinkled the corners of his eyes, sending her pulse into overdrive. "Any woman who orders a salad, French fries, a Reuben sandwich and a slice of chocolate layer cake could never be called boring."

"You were buying. I was hungry," she said. "I really like food."

"So do I."

They had something in common. Two things if you considered their dependency on oxygen. They also didn't have dads. Three things. She could probably find a few more.

What was she doing? And then she realized…

Adam Noble might appear to be a brainless surfer dude with an arrogant streak as wide as the Texas panhandle, but he wasn't. She was attracted to him. Not only his looks, but also the way he listened and talked to her. It wasn't the same as with Rob, but nice. Almost…better.

Not better, she corrected. Different. Still…

Falling for him would be a disaster of epic proportions.

She had to keep reminding herself that.

Over and over again until it sunk in.

There wasn't room in her life or her heart for someone like Adam Noble.

Walking Megan back to the wardrobe department, Adam couldn't remember the last time he'd enjoyed a meal so much. Not the food, though it wasn't bad, but the company. Something about Megan Calhoun put a big smile on his face. Being with her made him feel good. Not that he'd been down, but something seemed to be missing in his life lately. He couldn't quite explain it, except when he was at lunch with Megan he hadn't felt that way.

He glanced at her. She was the definition of low maintenance, something rare in this town. He appreciated that she ate real food and didn't seem concerned about calories or making sure she had the perfect forty-thirty-thirty percentages of protein, carbs and fat on her plate. Yet she wasn't overweight, though her baggy clothes suggested as much.

If he were looking for a girlfriend...

Whoa. A girlfriend was the last thing he needed. Wanted. A fling during a shoot was all he would commit to. Would a small-town girl be interested in a no-strings relationship? Given what her coworkers had said, probably not.

Unfortunately.

Megan's gaze bounced from one thing to the next, taking mental pictures. She was like a sponge soaking up the objects around her. Her interest and her excitement at the buildings, equipment and people they passed were palpable.

Very cute.

Adam couldn't believe she thought she was boring. Someone who was boring would never have accepted an internship so far from home. If anything, she wanted to be swept into an adventure, though she'd deny it. After all she'd been through, she deserved one.

The V between her eyebrows had returned during lunch and remained there. That bothered Adam. He wanted her to relax, not tense up around him. "You okay?"

"Full after such a big lunch, but otherwise fine." Megan stared at a photo shoot. The photographer's assistant rearranged lights. "Everywhere I look I see something new. This studio is a world unto itself."

Her wide-eyed wonder appealed to Adam. "It's like living in a bubble during a shoot. The set becomes your entire life."

"I suppose there are worse places to be."

He thought of some of the apartments and trailer parks he'd lived in as a child. "Much worse."

She spun, looking up, down, all around. "It's almost as if you can feel it."

Megan was so much fun to watch. He'd been as excited as he was nervous when he worked on his first film, but he hadn't wanted others to know that. "Feel what?"

"Movie magic."

The awe in her voice wrapped around his heart like a hug. "Some of that magic will get lost once you see what goes on during a shoot. It doesn't seem quite so real with all the lights, cameras and equipment around."

"Maybe, but I'm sure when I see it on the screen I'll feel the same way."

"You like movies."

She nodded. "I love them. Nothing better than losing myself for a couple of hours in this world or another universe."

"You'll have to go to Mann's Chinese Theatre. A perfect place for a movie buff."

"It's on my list of sights to see."

He remembered her saying she was a planner. "That's one way not to miss anything."

She stared up at him. "Let me guess. You're a shoot-from-the-hip kind of guy."

He nodded.

"Most guys are."

He wondered what kind of guys she knew, who she had dated or was dating. None of his business. "I have an agent, a manager and an assistant who make lists. Two are men."

"An entourage of list makers, huh?"

Megan sure had a pretty smile. "Entourages are important in this town. Lots to keep track of with me."

"I'm sure keeping track of you is a full-time job," she teased.

His agent might agree with her. "Don't believe everything you read. At least half of what they print is a lie or exaggeration."

She raised a finely arched brow. "Only half?"

He grinned. "Three-quarters."

"The juicier, the better, I assume."

"Scandalous headlines sell better," he admitted. "The stuff

they write is unreal. I haven't lived like a monk, but I'm not some dog chasing after every female in heat."

"You're nicer than I thought you would be."

"Thank you. I think."

"It's a compliment."

That was something. "I can be nice, but I'm a big flirt, too. You know guys. We always have to try."

Megan stopped walking. "Always?"

The V deepened. Something was bothering her. "Pretty much."

"Hypothetically, if a guy doesn't try…"

"Then he's already got a girl or…"

Megan stared up at him with rapt attention. "Or?"

She had to be talking about herself. Adam cocked a brow. "Hypothetically?"

"Not exactly." She bit her lip. "Maybe you could help me understand this. Him."

Knew it. And Adam didn't like it. Territorial? Maybe, even if it made no sense. He wanted to know who the guy was. Someone she'd known a long time or someone she just met. Whoever he was sounded like a fool. Megan wouldn't have to ask Adam twice to fool around with her. "Sounds like you've been banished to friend zone."

"*Banished* is the right word. I could walk around naked and he wouldn't notice me."

Adam would notice. But her words made him wonder what kind of friend this guy was. "Have you walked around naked in front of him?"

She drew back, as if horrified by the question. "Of course not."

Good. Adam didn't want her to be taken advantage of. "I've got to be honest with you. Most guys will fool around with female friends if given the opportunity."

Her shoulders slumped. She blew out a puff of air.

Adam didn't like seeing her look so deflated. "Not what you wanted to hear."

"Nope."

"There are two other possibilities," Adam offered.

Megan perked up.

"The guy could be superconservative and religious."

"He goes to church only for funerals and weddings."

If Megan knew that much about him, he couldn't be a new guy. "Then he's gay."

She glared at Adam. "Rob is not gay."

"So this hypothetical has a name. The same name as your best friend from high school."

"Yes, and trust me, Rob likes girls. Women. He's dated several. Just not me." She sighed. "Forget I said anything."

Her dejected tone bothered Adam. "I can't forget now that it's out there."

"You're an actor," she countered. "Pretend."

"I can do that for you. Or…"

She sighed. "I'm not sure I'm ready to hear more. Why don't we say goodbye here? I can find my way back."

He wasn't about to let her get away from him that easily. "A gentleman always escorts his date home."

"I'm not your date."

"I thought you were going to say I wasn't a gentleman."

The corners of her mouth lifted. "The thought may have crossed my mind."

Good. She was back to joking. "You, Megan Calhoun, are one of a kind."

"Next you'll say I have a great personality."

"I don't know you well enough to say that." Even if he was thinking it. "But I will tell you if your best friend, this Rob guy, has stuck you in friend zone, you're better off without him because he's got to be a total idiot."

She started to speak, then stopped herself. "Rob is smart. He's an engineer."

Adam wished she wasn't so quick to stand up for the guy. She deserved better than to wait around for some bozo, one that lived in another state, to wake up. There were plenty of men here in L.A. to choose from. "Being book smart doesn't apply here. Find another guy. Someone who'll appreciate you. Spoil you. Kiss you until you can't see straight."

Her lips parted.

With another woman he might think that was an invitation for a kiss. With Megan, he couldn't be sure of anything.

She eyed him suspiciously. "Exactly where am I going to find a guy like that?"

"He could be right under your nose," Adam said. "But if you keep waiting to get out of friend zone with Rob, you'll probably miss him."

CHAPTER FIVE

ON SUNDAY afternoon, Adam returned to the lot. The studio was the last place he needed to be, but he wanted to check out his trailer.

He glanced around seeing his favorite things that would help him relax in between takes and during downtimes—weights, a pull-up bar and video game consoles. "Looks good. Thanks."

Veronica Tully, his personal assistant, stared at her tablet. She was the definition of efficiency. "You've been invited to two parties tonight as well as a special event at the Wilshire. If you're going to show up, no worries, but if not I'll send your regrets."

With his first call on the set early Tuesday morning, Adam should make the most of tonight. But the thought of hanging with the usual crowd didn't appeal to him.

Parts of his character, Maxwell Caldecott, must be rubbing off on Adam. Forget clubbing and partying. Hardworking, idealistic, family man wannabe, Maxwell attended formal events, the kind that required tuxedos or jackets and ties. Anything to prove his worth to the high-society wife he loved more than life. Too bad she was going to end up making the Wicked Witch seem more like the tooth fairy.

Staying home didn't appeal to Adam, either. He'd spent last night working on lines. Still…

Sometimes he had to show up at events and parties because that was expected of him due to starring in a certain role or wanting to be cast in an upcoming project. He'd "dated" costars because the producer or studio wanted to drum up publicity. It was all business, all the time. "Any reason I should attend?"

Veronica scanned her tablet. "No."

"Send my regrets," he said without any further hesitation.

"I'll book a table for you for dinner. Seven-thirty," Veronica said with the same competency she'd shown since she started working for him a year and a half ago.

Adam didn't want to be tied into any plans. He'd have enough of that during the shoot. "Thanks, but I'll figure out something myself. Take the rest of the day and tomorrow off. It'll be crazy around here starting Tuesday."

"Thanks, boss." She walked toward the door, then glanced back. "If you need me…"

"You're only a text away."

So was someone else, Adam realized. Megan. As Veronica exited the trailer, he whipped out his cell phone and typed.

Working today?

He didn't know why Megan kept popping into his mind. No, he knew. Someone different and new was more fun than the same old same. She was probably out and about, checking off sights she wanted to see on her list. He'd bet she had actual lists, either on paper or her computer. No doubt a copy on her cell phone.

A beep sounded. A text had arrived. He checked his cell phone. A reply from Megan.

Yes, but almost finished.

Too bad. Adam was hoping she'd been able to have fun today. He typed.

Running an errand or at the lot?

Lot.

Her reply was almost instantaneous. He smiled. If they were so close, they could be talking instead of texting. An idea formed in his head. He typed another message.

All work and no play…

Hahaha.

Laughter wasn't the reply Adam wanted. He wanted her to say she was up for some playtime. Fun. He'd try again.

Let me show you some sights when you're finished.

No reply came. That was weird considering how quickly she'd answered back before. He typed some more.

Lived in L.A. area my entire life. I like playing tour guide.

Time dragged. He checked out the shelf full of video games. Some good titles.

His cell phone beeped. Finally. He read the text.

Too tired. Not up for fighting freeways and crowds.

Adam knew she must be tired, but he didn't like the idea of her being alone. He remembered what being the new kid was like, whether at school or at a studio. It could be lonely, even if others were around. People had helped him when he first went to work on movies. He wanted to do the same with Megan. Tonight was the perfect time, possibly the only time, to do it. And being with her this evening beat any of his alternatives.

His thumbs tapped the touchscreen.

Understand. But I know the perfect place. Very relaxing. We can make it an early night.

As Adam waited for a reply, anticipation built. Must be the challenge. Few women kept him waiting. Most simply fell at his feet, seeing him whenever he wanted to see them. Having women willing to revolve their lives around him was convenient, but it made Adam uncomfortable because that was what his mom did for her man of the moment. He couldn't picture Megan doing that.

The seconds ticked into minutes. He imagined her weighing the pros and the cons, the V between her eyes deepening into almost parallel lines, as she made a list. Perhaps a mental one, or she might even be jotting one down. He wouldn't put it past Megan. But he still hoped she said...

Another beep. He glanced at the screen.

Sure.

Adam pumped his hand. "Yes."
Another message immediately followed.

Where do you want to meet?

Picking her up would be easiest, but that might seem like too much of a date. Like it wasn't a date, a voice mocked. Ignoring it, he typed.

Griffith Park Observatory parking lot. Five o'clock.

Okay. See you then.

A satisfied feeling flowed through Adam. He couldn't wait to see Megan. Once the shoot started, things would be hectic for both of them. He wanted to make the most of tonight.

And he would.

The sun dropped lower toward the horizon, filling the sky with satiny tendrils of yellow and pink. Megan sat on a blanket on the lawn area of the Griffith Observatory. Adam sat next to her. In his jeans, long-sleeved red shirt with a surfer logo on the front and an L.A. Dodgers hat with the brim pulled low, he still didn't look like an average guy. But no one walking passed them recognized him.

The scent of the grass filled the air, mingling with the smells from the delicious dinner Adam had brought. A good thing they'd taken a short hike through Griffith Park when they arrived. She didn't think she could do it now after eating fried chicken, corn on the cob, sweet potato fries and the flakiest buttermilk biscuits she'd ever tasted.

Megan stared at the view of Los Angeles, including the iconic Hollywood sign. "I always thought everything in L.A. was flashy and loud. Glad to see I was wrong."

"This is an oasis in the city. My mom and I used to come here when I was younger."

She wondered what Adam was like as a kid, probably a daredevil even then. "Thank you for suggesting we come here. It's so nice. The park. The view. The food."

"The company."

She smiled up at him. "That, too."

And so romantic. Better not go there. They were friends. Only friends.

Except being with Adam wasn't the same as hanging out with her friends. A strange undercurrent kept things from feeling comfy and cozy like when she was with Rob. With Adam, she felt kind of prickly and off balance. She had no idea what might happen next. Funny, but that didn't bother her as much as she thought it would.

Megan put her arms behind her so she could lean back and support her weight. Her hand brushed Adam's. Heat and tingles erupted from the point of contact. She straightened. "Sorry."

"No worries."

Megan was worried. She couldn't control her body's reactions to him. Even the slightest touch sent her insides aquiver. Not good.

He removed a white cardboard box from the picnic basket, then opened the lid. "I hope you saved room for dessert."

Megan peeked inside to see two big chocolate cupcakes with fluffy white icing. The mouthwatering scent added two more inches to her hips. She took one, anyway. Focusing on dessert was better than thinking about Adam. "No matter how full I am, there's always room for a cupcake."

Laughter filled his eyes.

"What?" she asked.

"It isn't often I meet a woman who enjoys food the way you do."

Megan shifted uncomfortably. She wanted to fit in with everyone else, find where she belonged, but she wasn't about to starve herself to do it. Especially when cupcakes were involved. "It's a love-hate relationship. Most women enjoy food, but they hate the calories."

"You don't seem worried about calories."

"I'm not," she admitted. "I might have been a size zero for about a week when I was twelve. But as long as I'm fit and healthy why not eat?"

He held a cupcake. "I agree completely."

She bit into hers. The vanilla frosting, creamy and sweet, filled her mouth. So tasty. The cake was light and chocolaty. Perfect, like Adam.

Megan stiffened. He wasn't perfect. Okay, maybe physically. She'd concede that much. But other things considered— stability and respectability—not even close. Adam might not be as big a show-off as she'd first thought, but he was reckless and a daredevil. Totally wrong for her. She stared at her cupcake.

"You look a million miles away," Adam said.

She turned her head. The intensity in his green eyes made her breath catch.

"I'm back." She took another bite of the delicious cupcake. "You said you came here with your mother."

He nodded. "We didn't have a lot of money when I was growing up. This was one place we could afford. Admission is free except for the planetarium show."

"A bargain for the beautiful views."

"Wait until you see inside and look at the sky through a telescope. I used to…"

The wistful look in his eyes intrigued Megan. She leaned toward him, eager to hear what he was going to say. "What?"

"Dream about being an astronaut."

More adventure and thrills. Not surprising. "You wanted to fly the space shuttle."

"No." Now that surprised her. "I didn't want to be a pilot, but a mission specialist. A scientist."

To be a scientist meant he had to like science. Her first impression of him being a dumb jock had been way off base. This only reaffirmed how far off.

Megan imagined Adam wearing a white lab coat. He would look good no matter what he wore. "You would have been the hottest scientist ever. Every female research assistant would have wanted to work on your project."

On him!

Adam grinned. "Thanks."

"But I'll be honest, you would look even hotter in a spacesuit."

"I've worn one before. I played an astronaut in a movie. The best part was experiencing zero gravity during a parabolic flight. Talk about wild. You would have liked it."

"I suppose doing somersaults in midair would be fun as long as you didn't hit something while you were floating around."

"Everything is controlled. Very safe."

Being an actor gave Adam the opportunity to experience unique things that an average person like herself didn't get to do. That had to be fun for him. "Playing an astronaut in a movie would be a lot safer than actually being blasted into space."

Mischief gleamed in his eyes. "Nothing wrong with a little danger."

"Says the surfer who rides the biggest wave out there."

He raised his hands in the air like he had won a close race. "And conquers the biggest wave."

"Long-term, my money's on the wave."

Adam shrugged. "The rush is worth the risk."

"I'll take my chances on dry ground."

"There's rock climbing."

"Not my thing," she admitted. "I'm not a big fan of heights."

"So no skydiving or BASE jumping."

"Nope." She'd never done anything like that, nor did she plan on it. "I like to keep my feet firmly planted on the ground. I'm addicted to breathing, not adrenaline."

"Come on, you can't tell me you're totally risk adverse."

"It's true."

"If it were, you wouldn't be here."

Megan drew back, feeling suddenly exposed. Most people took what she said without looking deeper. Even Rob. She might not have known Adam long, but the things she kept hidden from the world seemed somehow visible to him. She didn't like it. "You mean here with you?"

"I'm not dangerous."

Oh, yes, he was. She swallowed.

"I was talking about your internship," Adam continued before she could say anything. "You left your family and friends to move to Los Angeles. That's not exactly taking the safe path."

Moving to a new town wouldn't kill or injure her the way his risks would. At least she hoped not. "There aren't many job opportunities for costume designers in Larkville. None unless you count the annual Christmas pageant at the community church. They've used the same costumes for years."

"What about another city like Austin? They're well-known in filmmaking circles."

She'd had this discussion with Rob. "Nothing beats being in Hollywood if you want to be in the film industry. Lots more opportunities."

"That's true," Adam said. "A great place to gain experience."

Maybe that was why Rob had encouraged her to take the internship. Once she had experience, she would be able to move to Austin. "But relocating for a job isn't the same as risking my neck trying some extreme sport."

"Maybe not, but it still could be life changing."

She stifled a yawn. "Time will tell."

"You're tired."

Nodding, she wiped her mouth with a napkin and put the cupcake wrapper with the other trash. "It's been a long week."

"Let's relax and watch the sunset before heading into the observatory."

With her stomach full and her eyelids heavy, Megan stretched out her jean-clad legs and leaned back on her elbows. "Sounds like a plan."

"That doesn't look comfortable." He moved back until he was behind her, his legs outstretched alongside hers. "Lean back."

Her heart lodged in her throat, as if she'd swallowed an entire box of cupcakes whole. This didn't seem like a friendly gesture, but a come-on. "I…"

He slipped his hands under her arms and scooted her against him so her back rested against his chest. "This has got to be more comfortable."

Only slightly better than walking on hot coals. Every single muscle knotted. Should she pull away or…?

"Relax." He kneaded her shoulders. "You're so tense."

Warmth and more tingles pulsated through her. If Adam decided to give up acting, he would make a fortune as a masseur.

"That's a little better," he said.

Yes and no. The man had magic hands. The tightness in her shoulders loosened, quickly melting beneath his skilled fingers, but his touch heated the blood flowing through her veins. Uh-oh. She could not allow herself to make a mistake here. "Much better. Thanks. You can stop now."

"In a minute."

A minute, huh? Megan could handle that. She started counting. One-Mississippi, two-Mississippi, three…

* * *

Megan was asleep. Her entire body was finally relaxed. Her chest rose and fell evenly.

With his left arm around Megan, Adam felt an odd sense of contentment. He'd never brought a date here before. This had always been his and his mom's favorite place, but bringing Megan felt right. Special.

One of her curls tickled Adam's nose. He inhaled the scent of her shampoo, fruity and sweet.

"Wheeeeee."

A little boy squealed as he toddled across the grass while his mom chased after him. Beyond them, on the path, an older couple walked hand in hand. A teenager jogged to catch up to his friends heading toward the observatory.

Megan shifted in his arms. He glanced down at her. She was wearing lipstick, a natural-looking pink shade. He'd never noticed her wearing makeup before.

A serene smile graced her full lips. Was she dreaming? Of him?

This morning he would have said no way, but he wasn't sure now. She'd agreed to spend the evening with him and didn't protest his massaging her shoulders. She might be a little more dazzled than she would admit, but that didn't stop her from acting naturally around him. She didn't try to impress him. Nor try to seduce and flirt with him. She was herself and let him be himself. A rare occurrence. One he liked very much.

Adam didn't think Megan was as practical as she claimed to be. Planners could have an adventurous streak. He would like the chance to bring hers out. He wanted to see her face light up with joy, to hear her laugh from the gut. If only she would let him…

He brushed a corkscrew curl off her face. Her pale skin contrasted with her brown curly hair.

A modern-day Sleeping Beauty or Snow White.

All she needed was a kiss.

Bad idea.

Each time they touched, Megan about jumped out of her

skin, suggesting she was attracted to him. But she was deny-ing her interest in him. She was trying to banish him to friend zone because she had her sights set on another guy.

Adam could overcome her resistance. He had no doubt about that. Yet even if he was tempted to brush his lips against hers and steal a kiss, he wouldn't.

Adam might be charming, but he wasn't a prince. He was more like the huntsman. Megan's heart wasn't safe with him. She might not be his normal type, but the more time he spent with her, the more he liked her. One kiss might lead to more and that could take them to the wrong place. The last thing he wanted to do was hurt Megan.

Listening to her talk about her feelings for Rob, hearing about her plans, told Adam that she was a forever type of woman. He wasn't that kind of guy. Kissing her was out of the question. Even if he might want a...taste.

She shifted positions, turning so her cheek rested against his chest. Her soft-in-all-the-right-places curves pressed against him.

A flame ignited deep within him.

Adam swallowed around the lump in his throat. Better there than in his jeans. That would be hard...difficult to explain if Megan woke up.

He focused on the other people around them. It didn't help.

He thought about the scene he'd been working on earlier that day. He'd kept screwing up one line. He repeated the words in his head, messing up again. But at least his temperature hadn't skyrocketed into the danger zone. He went over the line in his head. Again and again. He spoke the words aloud.

Megan stirred.

Damn, he should have been quieter. At least he'd managed to stave off being embarrassed by his attraction to her.

A gasp escaped her parted lips. Wide eyes stared up at him.

He smiled at her. "Sleeping Beauty awakes."

Her cheeks turned a cute shade of pink. She bolted upright. "I fell asleep."

He missed the feel of her warmth and softness against him. "You were tired."

She wouldn't meet his eyes. "I'm sorry."

"Don't apologize." He didn't want her to be embarrassed. "I'm sorry I woke you. I was practicing a line."

To stop himself getting too turned on. *Real classy, Noble.* A good thing Megan didn't need to know that piece of info.

"Do you need help?" she offered.

Yes, he would love her help, but not with the line. "Another time."

"Just tell me when." She brushed strands of hair off her face. "That's the least I can do to thank you for being my bed while I napped."

If only they could be in bed together… Nope. Not going there. "You're welcome. I'm happy to oblige anytime."

"Anytime Eva's not around," Megan clarified.

She would bring that up. Adam wished he could put her at ease about her internship. He enjoyed flirting with her whether it went anywhere or not. "Even if Eva strolled by, what could she say? It's not like we're naked with our legs and arms tangled amid the sheets and each other."

The images had been rolling around in his head ever since she'd mentioned the word *bed*.

Megan cleared her throat. "No, you're right. It's not like that at all."

Too bad, Adam thought. That image held a certain appeal.

"A good thing or I'd be out an internship," Megan continued.

"True," he said.

But what a way to go.

Forget movie magic, Megan had gotten a taste of real magic tonight with Adam. She stood next to him by her car in the parking lot, feeling rested and content.

Above her in the night sky, stars twinkled, the same stars she and Adam had stared at through the telescope at the observatory. "I thought that was a shooting star."

"Shooting star. Satellite," he said. "Not a lot of difference."

"You can't wish upon a satellite."

The lights from the parking lot combined with the brim of his baseball cap cast shadows on his face. The proverbial tall, dark and handsome. "You can make a wish on anything you want."

"No, you can't," she countered. "You need a coin and a fountain or wishing well. Birthday candles or…"

He grinned wryly. "I didn't know there was a wish rule book."

Megan gave him a look. "You can't make up your own wishing rules."

"For your information I've made plenty of wishes up here," he said. "Granted, they were on stars, but none were shooting across the sky."

She wondered what Adam would wish for. He had looks, money, fame and a great career. Nothing was missing from his life. "Have any come true?"

"Yes," he said without any hesitation. "So there's nothing from stopping you from making a wish now."

"Only if you make one, too."

"I'm always up for making wishes," he said to her surprise.

Megan thought he would put up more of a fight. She hadn't taken Adam as the fanciful type, but the more time she spent with him, the more she realized how much she didn't know about him and wanted to know.

"Close your eyes," Adam said.

"You implied there isn't a rule book."

"Now is not the time to be logical." He tapped the tip of her nose with his fingertip. "Close them."

She did. "Are yours closed?"

"Yes," he said. "Now make a wish."

I wish I could spend more time with Adam.

Wait. The words sounding in her head had come out of nowhere. Her eyes sprung open. Spending time with Adam wouldn't be smart if she wanted to impress Eva. Megan grimaced.

She knew what she should have wished for—a permanent costume design job. Or Rob to see her as more than a friend. Or finding the place she belonged. Or... Her shoulders sagged.

Instead, she'd made a stupid wish. For something she didn't want or need. For someone who wasn't a part of her life and never would be. A do-over wish was definitely in order.

Adam's eyes opened. She realized he'd taken a long time to make his wish.

"Did you make one?" he asked.

"Yes." Even if it was a total waste of a wish. Oh, well. Her wishes had never come true. This one wouldn't, either. "You?"

"I made a good one."

He sounded happy. She was tempted to ask him what he wished for, but realizing he'd want to know hers kept Megan quiet. No way was she admitting her wish to him. To anyone.

This seemed like a perfect time to say good-night. They couldn't stand here for hours, making wishes or staring at each other. She needed sleep and clarity. "I should get going. Thanks for tonight."

"It doesn't have to end."

Megan's pulse kicked up a notch. She didn't want the night to end. Being with Adam made her feel special, as if for the past couple of hours the universe revolved around her. She knew it was the way he treated everybody—making her feel like the most important and only person in the world—but she didn't care. It felt so good. Her dad had made her feel so unique and special. With him gone, she'd wondered if she would ever feel that way again.

"There are plenty of other sights to see at night," Adam added.

His trailer? Her pulse sprinted as if she were running a hundred-yard dash.

Uh-oh. Time to slow down. No sense getting carried away over a pleasant evening. Adam had admitted to being a flirt, but she shouldn't go too far hanging out with him. Definitely time to call it a night.

As she removed her car keys from her purse, metal jingled.

"I have an early call time tomorrow morning." The words sounded flat even to her ears. She needed to sound more enthusiastic. She had come to Hollywood for her career, not to be crushing on a movie star who had millions of women lusting after him. She forced a smile. "Lots to prepare for Tuesday's call."

"Strong work ethic. I like that."

"Something my dad instilled in us. Me."

"It's an admirable trait."

Megan couldn't drum up any excitement over Adam's compliment. He may have been interested in her enough to flirt, but she wasn't hot enough for him to put in more effort and pursue. Being friends seemed to be okay with him.

Disappointment shot through her. Foolish, she knew, because friends were all they could be given her internship. And Rob. Megan couldn't forget about Rob. But spending time with Adam tonight gave her a glimpse of what being a princess must be like. Usually she felt like one of the ugly stepsisters, not Cinderella. Megan didn't want the feeling to end even if it were for the best. "Thanks again."

He wrapped his arms around her in a big bear hug. "Thank you for tonight."

The scent of him filled her nostrils. Musky and spicy and oh-so-male. Her cheek pressed against his chest, his heart beating in her ear. She hugged back, wanting to soak up his warmth. If only it could last for a little longer.

He released her.

She forced herself to let go of him.

Adam's gaze locked on hers. She wasn't experienced when it came to men, but she recognized the desire shining in his eyes. Her blood pressure spiraled into the red zone.

He looked like he wanted to kiss her.

Megan wanted him to kiss her.

His mouth was so close to hers, mere inches away. His warm breath, sweet with a hint of chocolate from the cupcakes, caressed her face.

She parted her lips in invitation.

Kiss me.

A wish. A plea.

He drew back slightly. "Drive safe on the way home."

Her heart dropped to her feet. He was saying good-night, not trying to kiss her. She cleared her dry throat. "You, too."

The two words were all she could manage.

"See you on Tuesday," he said.

Not if Megan could help it. She'd never had this kind of reaction to a friend before, not even Rob. The less she saw of Adam, the better. He made her feel entirely out of control.

She wasn't a swooning, obsessed fan, wanting a one-night stand with her idol. She was a professional. Okay, an intern, but if she wanted a permanent job she had to stay focused and not think about Adam Noble.

Not now, not ever.

CHAPTER SIX

ADAM loved shooting. Stepping into a role and losing himself in a character were second only to the adrenaline rush of succeeding at something difficult and dangerous. But life on the set was like moving from an aquarium to a fishbowl. His world became smaller and more visible. At least to the cast and crew.

That was a small price to pay to do what he loved.

Adam parked near the set. One of the perks of being a movie star was a reserved parking spot. His car was one of three vehicles in the VIP lot. Not surprising given the sun was just now clearing the horizon. He liked arriving early to give himself time to relax and prepare.

He always started his day with a cup of coffee from the refreshment table. Craft Services put out a spread of snacks and drinks to tide them over between the catered meals they were fed.

One of the electricians shouted a greeting.

Adam waved.

Spending twelve to fourteen hours with the same group of people gave him a chance to get to know the cast and crew well. But only a week in, he knew this production would be different because of two women—Megan Calhoun and Lane Gregory.

One was as sweet as a cupcake. He'd had barely caught sight of Megan since shooting began. But she'd been on his mind and in his dreams since last Sunday night. Two places no woman belonged. Thinking about sex was one thing. With

Megan, it was different. Okay, he might have thought about what she looked like naked and sleeping with her, but he'd also been imagining her pretty smile and her captivating eyes. Adam didn't have time to dwell on those things, however appealing. He needed to focus on his feelings, rather Maxwell's feelings, for his wife, Calliope. She was the only woman who could take up residence in his thoughts.

The other was his costar, Lane Gregory. She was the best of old Hollywood and new, but the woman was relentless in her pursuit of, well, him. Attention, gifts, innuendos. Adam had taken to hiding in his trailer whenever he could, something he rarely did while shooting. He preferred being where the action was. A good thing Lane wasn't an early riser.

"You're late," Lou, who worked for Craft Services, said. "I thought you might have slept in this morning."

"And miss the first pot of coffee? No way." Adam greeted the man with a handshake. "How did your daughter's softball game turn out?"

Lou grinned. "She hit the cycle. They won six-two."

"Excellent," Adam said. "There could be a scholarship in her future."

"Hope so." Lou handed him a steaming cup and a blueberry muffin, nicely warmed with a pat of butter softening on top of it. "Your standing order, sir."

"Thanks."

As Adam turned, he caught the scent of perfume wafting in the air. Not any perfume. Lane's.

Damn. She must have figured out his morning routine.

Maybe he could ditch her before she saw him. The costume department was nearby. He could sneak in and see if Megan was there. Interns always got the crappy call times. He wouldn't mind saying hi to her.

An oh-so-appealing image of her filled his mind. He'd missed seeing her.

On second thought, as tempting as paying her a visit might sound, he'd better not. On his mind was one thing. Under his skin was another. That was the one place he didn't allow a woman. It was safer that way.

"So it's true about you being an early bird." Some men might consider Lane Gregory's breathy voice sexy. Adam had at one time. But now the sound grated on his nerves. "I thought if I got here early enough we might be able to…rehearse in my trailer."

He should have gone to see Megan.

No way did he want to be alone with Lane. Not without a bodyguard. Maybe two. He might be strong, but the woman was dangerous. And not in a good way. "I have a few things I need to do."

Lane was beautiful. He'd give her that. Her long blond hair, porcelain skin and blue eyes were the envy of many women. Her curvy figure enticed men. She smiled coyly. "I can think of a few things we could do together."

Not in this lifetime. Adam pointed to her left hand where a huge diamond, iceberg-size, shimmered beneath the morning sun. "I doubt your fiancé would appreciate that."

Adam sipped his coffee. He needed to be alert to handle Lane's flirting.

She moved closer. "I doubt he'd mind if our rehearsing made the chemistry onscreen stronger."

Bull. He stepped back to put some distance between them. Just look at Rhys Rogers. The young actor's career was DOA thanks to "rehearsing" with Lane, and Hugh Wilstead's not-in-the-least-bit-understanding response. The studio head had the Midas touch and the respect of the industry. When Hugh spoke, everyone listened. No way would Adam cross him, not for a roll in the sack with Lane, not for anyone.

Lane, however, lived in a different reality. She'd grown up in the movie industry. She was spoiled and pampered and expected the world to fall at her feet. Pretty much the exact opposite of someone like Megan. He would have to try another tact. "Lane, beautiful, talented, Lane. Look at you. Look at me. All we have to do is stare at each other and the screen will sizzle with chemistry."

She gave him a sultry look. "Why not rehearse until passion explodes?"

"We'd end up with an R-rating or NC-17."

"I wouldn't mind."

Adam would. He wanted this film to be the best it could be, but there were limits to what he would do to achieve that goal. Lane was one of them. "Nothing personal, but I don't mess around with married or engaged women."

"Honorable. Dare I say noble?" She smirked. "But rules are meant to be broken."

"Some rules, yes," he admitted. "Not this one."

She winked. "We'll see about that."

She pranced away, her hips swaying seductively.

Adam was usually up for a fling with his costars, but Lane's engagement was only one reason he didn't want to sleep with her. She was all about artifice and deception. The total opposite of someone fresh and honest like…

Megan.

She stood outside the costume department. She wore a green jacket, jeans and canvas shoes. The shoes sparkled. Those were different than the sneakers she'd been wearing before. A black trendy-looking messenger bag hung on her shoulder. He hadn't seen that before, either. But her wild curls were still piled on top of her head. He wondered if she ever wore her hair down.

She had her cell phone pressed against her ear and a big smile on her face. Adam remembered the way she'd looked at him at the observatory. He'd thought she might want him to kiss her. But while waiting for another sign, he'd remembered his decision not to kiss her.

He wondered who was making her smile. Maybe that idiot best friend of hers.

Adam bit into his blueberry muffin to mask the bitterness souring his tongue.

Time to head back to his trailer. He needed to review his lines, not think about some woman who wanted another guy.

Walking away, Adam glanced over his shoulder. Megan was

still on the phone, but she was no longer smiling. She looked…
concerned. Maybe even upset.

Unease balled in his stomach.

Man, he was being stupid. No reason to overreact. Megan
was simply talking on the phone. So what if her smile had fal-
tered for a moment? It could be her boss or her landlord. Her
business wasn't his business. He should get out of here. Now.

Except his feet wouldn't budge. A protective instinct, the
same he'd felt whenever his mom used to introduce him to a
new "uncle," sprang to life.

The look on Megan's face, the way she ducked her head,
bothered Adam. It didn't matter who was on the other end of
the call. He didn't like the idea of anyone upsetting her.

She was too sweet, too nice.

This might not be his business, but Adam didn't want to
leave her on her own if she was upset. And he wouldn't. He
didn't have to be anywhere for another hour and a half.

He positioned himself at a table where he could see Megan
more clearly. This was as good as any other place to enjoy his
muffin. He took a bite and watched her.

Megan stood outside the costume department so happy to hear
from Rob. Not a text, but an actual phone call. She hadn't spoken to him in over a week. His texting had been erratic, too.

"It's good to talk to you, Meg," he said.

Her heart swelled with affection. With Rob in her life, she
would never be one of these people who died and her body
wasn't found for months because no one noticed she was missing. "I know. It's been insane here. Crazy busy. I've never
worked so hard in my life."

"Have you met anybody?"

"Oh, I've met lots of people." Megan listed the various crew
members she'd befriended. She thought about Adam, too, even
though she'd wanted to avoid him. Thankfully, he hadn't been
around much except during shoots. She'd seen him only in

passing. He would wave or nod in her general direction. The way he'd done to others when they'd had lunch at the cafeteria.

Megan should be happy he treated her like everyone else and wasn't going out of his way for her. That was what she wanted. Distance. Except staying away from him and being treated the same as others didn't feel as good as she thought it would. She no longer felt…special. Silly, but true.

"That's great you're making friends," Rob said. "But I wanted to know if you met a guy yet."

She let the words sink in, unsure what to say or think. This was the first time Rob had ever mentioned her and another guy. She didn't like it. "You mean someone to, um, date?"

"Yes."

Adam popped into her head. Too bad the only thing "date" and "Adam" had in common were the number of letters in the words. She pressed her lips together. "No, but I've been, um, busy."

Though others, including Kenna and Rosie, had been flirting with guys since the shoot started. Megan couldn't help but compare each man she met to Adam. So far none came close to the friendly, handsome actor.

"Too bad," Rob said.

Weird. He sounded…disappointed. "What about you? Have you met anyone?"

"Actually, I have."

The air rushed from her lungs. She nearly dropped the phone. "Really? I mean… That's great." She tried to sound interested, happy. "Who is she?"

"Someone you know. Knew. Pru Bradford."

Megan recognized the name. She tried to place it. "Prissy Prudence from fifth grade? The girl who never wore anything but frilly dresses and fancy shoes?"

"Yeah," Rob said. "She still wears dresses, but she's a lot prettier now. She works at an art gallery. She loves to cook, and you should see the things she knits. So talented."

Megan's heart plummeted to the pavement. Splat.

"She doesn't sound like your type at all." Meow. Megan's claws were showing. "You've never shown any interest in art." Not that Larkville had any "arts" to speak of. That was one thing that made her feel as if she were suffocating there. "Or knitting."

Or sewing. Her sewing.

"A couple of shirts Pru's made are hot."

"I've designed some hot dresses," Megan countered.

Ouch. That sounded kind of desperate.

"For who?" he asked.

She grimaced. "Me."

"I had no idea," Rob said.

That was because she'd kept the dresses a secret. She figured no one would like them so why open herself up to more criticism. "The local cattleman's dinner or the library dessert benefit don't exactly call for haute couture."

But it was more than that. People hadn't tried to understand her. The high school drama teacher had been a despot who wanted no input on costumes. The Larkville quilting bee didn't appreciate the ideas and creativity Megan brought to their gatherings. The entire town, especially her mother, had wanted to break Megan as if she were a wild mustang needing to be tamed.

"That's true," he agreed. "But I've got to admit, it's hard to picture you all dressed up with makeup and your hair done."

Rob saw her as Cinderella before her fairy godmother arrived, not a beautiful princess the prince wanted to marry. That stung. "We might have grown up together, but there are a few things you don't know about me."

"Yeah, it's been fun learning about Pru."

Ouch. Rob hadn't a clue. Megan blew out an exasperated puff of air. "I bet."

"I know what you should do," he said. "Find yourself a boyfriend so you can doll yourself up and wear one of your dresses."

Megan grimaced. First a date, now he wanted her to find a

boyfriend? Rob had parked her in friend zone and let the meter expire. She dug her toe into the asphalt. "I can't conjure up a date out of thin air."

"Have you thought about online dating?"

Yeah, right. She would be the one woman to end up catching the eye of an ax murderer or psychopath. "Not my style."

"There's a guy out there for you, Meg, I just know it."

Yeah, you.

But that wasn't looking likely now. Not as long as Prudence was in the picture. Megan thought about what Adam had said.

Find another guy. Someone who will appreciate you. Spoil you. Kiss you until you can't see straight.

She sighed. "For all I know he could be right under my nose."

Or on the opposite end of this telephone call.

"That's the spirit. I want you to be as happy as I am," he continued. "There's nothing better than starting fresh in a new town with a new job, new apartment, new girlfriend."

Her stomach roiled. Thank goodness she hadn't eaten breakfast yet or she might be sick. "Things are moving fast."

"Sometimes you just know."

His words speared her heart. She forced herself to breathe. "Sounds…serious."

"I really think Pru could be a keeper," he confessed.

Rob had never talked this way about a woman. Megan couldn't believe he was talking about Prissy Prudence. Okay, they'd been ten years old when she moved, but how much could a person change in twelve years?

Megan didn't want to know the answer. "Keep me posted."

"I will," he said. "I plan on bringing Pru to the Fall Festival in October. She hasn't been back to Larkville since her family moved away."

It was May and Rob was talking about October? Megan cleared her dry-as-sandpaper throat. "The more, the merrier."

Forget caffeine drinks. Megan needed to mainline chocolate to survive today.

"Pru loves going to the movies," Rob said. "Maybe we could visit you in L.A."

The thought of watching Rob and Pru hold hands and kiss made Megan nauseous. "I have a small studio apartment. It might be a little cramped."

"We don't mind."

Could things get any worse? She didn't want to know the answer to that, either.

"Pru would love to see some movie stars in person," Rob continued. "Adam Noble is her favorite."

At least Megan had something to contribute to the conversation. "Adam is the lead actor in the film I'm working on. He's a nice guy. Very friendly."

An excellent pillow and backrest, too.

"You know Adam Noble?" Rob sounded impressed.

That surprised her. He wasn't into movie stars. "We've met."

"Wow. That's so cool."

The excitement in his voice had Megan staring at the phone in disbelief. Who was this person on the phone and what had he done to her best friend?

"I have a brilliant idea," Rob said. "Pru's birthday is coming up. Could you get an autographed picture of Adam Noble for her?"

Seriously? Megan's shoulders couldn't sag any more or they'd be hitting the ground. She needed a T-shirt with the words *Sucks to Be Me!* imprinted on the front and *Doormat* on the back. "I don't know. When's her birthday?"

"July. It would mean a lot to me."

They could be broken up by then. Or engaged, an evil little voice whispered. "I'll, um, see what I can do."

"I can always count on you. Best buds forever."

Until some other woman clawed her talons into his heart and carried him away from her. Anxiety grabbed hold of her. "I should get going."

She would rather face an angry Firebreather than stay on the phone with Rob any longer.

"Good talking to you," he said. "I'm almost glad Pru was busy so I had time to call you on my break."

Almost? That wasn't a nice thing for Rob to say. Megan gritted her teeth. He'd always treated her like an all-star. Now she was second string. Telling him to dump the girl probably wouldn't be a smart move. She'd better think of something else to say. "You know me. Always there for my best bud."

"Don't forget about Adam Noble's autograph," Rob said. "If he could personalize it to Pru that would be awesome."

"Awesome," Megan repeated. What had Adam said when she used that word when they had lunch?

That's a strong adjective.

She supposed it would be awesome for Rob and Prudence.

Megan couldn't imagine a guy like Adam asking her to get his girlfriend something for birthday. He probably wouldn't get a woman a toolbox, either. That had been Rob's birthday present for her. Okay, she'd used a screwdriver to put together a table she bought. Still…

So. Not. Romantic.

But when you were a "best bud," romance didn't factor into gift selection. Anger surged. All her plans for a future with Rob were vaporizing. Plans or fantasies? The latter looked more likely at the moment.

"Text me and let me know when you have the autograph," Rob said.

Megan disconnected the call. Talking to Rob had drained what energy she had left.

"Good morning."

She jumped, startled to see Adam. What was he doing here so early?

"Here you go." He handed her a steaming cup of coffee. "What's going on? You look like you lost your best friend."

"I think I might have."

"Rob?"

"He thinks he found a keeper."

"That has to hurt."

She thought for a moment. "I'm more angry."

He smiled at her. "That's better than sad."

Nodding, she took a sip. The coffee was black. Strong. She choked. "I didn't realize you drank sludge."

"The stronger, the better. Especially on Fridays."

"I've been dragging since Wednesday."

"You'll get used to it."

"I have a feeling I'm going to have to get used to a lot of things."

"This must be messing up your plans."

"Wreaking havoc."

"Anything I can do to help," Adam offered.

She'd spilled most of the details about Rob. Might as well tell him everything so she would look like a loser only once. "Actually, there is. I don't know if it's against the rules or anything, but would you mind signing an autographed picture for Rob's girlfriend, Prudence? I mean, Pru. It's going to be a birthday gift from him. You're her favorite actor."

Adam's gaze narrowed. "He asked you to do this for him?"

Megan nodded, realizing how silly she must look.

His brow slanted. "Does Rob know how you feel about him?"

"Sort of."

"Say again?"

"Well, I once told him how I felt." The mortification of that still made her cringe even after all these years. "That didn't go over well. But I've dropped hints."

"Hints?"

She nodded. "He'll figure them out."

"And you still think the guy's smart?"

"Unless he's pretending to be oblivious."

Adam frowned. "You need to get away from Rob."

"He's in Texas."

"Doesn't matter where he is," Adam said. "You can do much better than someone like him."

"Maybe." But as she spoke the words her heart screamed, *Definitely!*

"How did he figure out we know each other?" Adam asked.

"I told Rob about you."

Adam's smile crinkled the corners of his eyes, sending her pulse rate into overdrive. "So what did you tell him? How much taller I am in real life? Or hotter? Or that I'm a very comfortable pillow?"

His lighthearted tone told Megan he was joking, but her cheeks warmed. Friend or not, Adam probably wasn't interested in hearing her whine about some other guy she was into. "I, um, told him you were starring in the film I was working on."

"The hotter and pillow comments might have made him jealous."

"Rob isn't the jealous type. He wants me to meet someone out here."

Adam raised his hand. "You met me."

"I mean a guy."

He flexed his arms, striking a he-man macho pose. "Do I look like a girl?"

She grinned. "No, but Rob was talking about a guy I could date."

Adam's mouth quirked. "So now I'm undateable."

Megan gave him a look. "You know what I mean."

"What?" He sounded surprised. "We went out. We could do it again."

"No, we can't."

"Because I'm the lead actor."

She nodded. "I keep waiting for Eva to give me the talk she gives everyone who works for her. But so far I've been spared."

No doubt Eva didn't think any movie star would be interested in a lowly intern from a nothing town in Texas.

"If I wasn't off-limits, would you go out with me?" he asked. "Say a real dinner at a restaurant, not a friendly picnic."

She remembered how romantic Adam had made everything

at the observatory and how close their lips had been when he hugged her. He'd seemed to want to kiss her, but backed away. She thought he wanted to be friends. Now she reveled in how he looked at her. He made her feel like Cinderella being asked to dance by the prince.

Her heart pounded. Heaven help her, she would say yes to him. No doubt about it. Megan swallowed around the lump in her throat. "You are off-limits so it's a moot question."

His frank appraisal made Megan want to cover her face with her hands and hide. But she kept her chin up and her posture straight, even if she was quivering inside.

"Fair enough," he said.

There was nothing fair about the way he made her forget everything, including Rob. Adam Noble was dangerous. Every instinct told her to get away from him. Now. "Thanks for the coffee. I have to go."

As Megan hustled into the costume department, she ignored the urge to glance over her shoulder and see if Adam was staring at her. She had to be realistic, not set herself up for more disappointment. Her hopes were already being dashed. She didn't need to let Adam in on the action, too. She didn't have a fairy godmother waiting to appear and wave a magic wand to make everything better. Fairy-tale endings didn't happen for girls like her. Even if, in her heart of hearts, she wished they did.

CHAPTER SEVEN

FRIDAY night, Megan turned down an invite to go out with the crew to a bar. She didn't want to be antisocial, but tiredness had finally gotten the best of her. Home in bed was the only place she belonged.

Saturday flew by. Sleeping in late. Laundry, napping. Her phone didn't ring or beep. She wanted to make the most of her free time. Rosie had told her once they were on location they might only get a day off a week.

By Sunday, Megan got antsy. She kept thinking about the lot, wondering how other people were spending today. Well, not all the crew. Adam.

She needed to have her head examined. Or better yet, find something to do so she would stop thinking about him.

Plopping onto a chair, she hit the power button on the television remote. Maybe she could find a movie to watch. A comedy would be good.

Megan surfed through the various channels. Adam appeared as the Roman god Neptune, standing on top of a wave. She let go of the remote.

Talk about gorgeous. She sighed.

What in the world was she doing? Megan was practically swooning over the guy. She turned off the TV.

No reason to go gaga over Adam Noble. Crushing on him was a total waste of time. He was the last person she should ever date, her internship aside.

She'd spent her entire life in the shadows. No one except her father and Rob had ever paid any real attention to her and made her feel important. She wanted to matter to someone, be an equal, not be overshadowed by his larger than life personality and in-the-spotlight career. Any woman who dated Adam, even his flings, ended up in the public eye, on view and scrutinized. No thanks. She'd had enough of that in Larkville.

Megan knew what would take her mind off Adam. She reached for her sketchpad and pencils.

Time to design a sundress worthy of the vintage fabric she'd purchased at a thrift store. The bodice seemed like a good place to start. Something fitted, a little retro looking to match the fabric. Slowly, the dress took shape both in her mind and on paper.

A knock sounded at the door.

Megan jumped. She glanced at the clock. Two hours had passed by. She'd been concentrating so hard she'd lost track of time. She rose. Probably Mrs. Hamilton from downstairs. Yesterday the elderly woman had needed help to locate her cat, Jack, who kept running away. Megan had found the orange tabby rummaging in the recyclable bin and returned him.

She opened the door. Shock rocketed through her.

Not Mrs. Hamilton. Adam.

He stood on her porch wearing a pair of board shorts, a plain white T-shirt and flip-flops. Somehow he made the casual clothing look like haute couture. His hair was mussed. Razor stubble covered his chin. He held a pair of sunglasses in one hand and a manila envelope in the other.

Megan clutched the doorknob. She tried to speak, but her tongue felt two sizes too big for her mouth. A million questions ran through her mind.

He greeted her with a charming smile that reached all the way to his clear green eyes. "Hello."

"Hi." She forced the word from her Sahara-dry mouth. "What are you doing here?"

He held up the envelope. "I have your autographed photo."

One question answered. Might as well ask the next one. "How did you find out where I live?"

"My assistant, Veronica."

That didn't explain how his assistant had gotten the address. Connections, perhaps?

Adam glanced over his shoulder. "Mind if I come in? I didn't see any paparazzi following me, but you never know."

She had more than enough reasons to not want him in her apartment, but she also didn't need a picture of her and Adam together finding its way to Eva.

Megan loosened her grip on the knob and stepped back. "Come on in."

As soon as Adam entered, his wide shoulders and six-foot height made the apartment feel ten times smaller. His male scent enveloped her. He smelled spicier today. Maybe he'd used a different soap or aftershave.

He looked around. "Nice place."

Thank goodness she'd cleaned up yesterday and made her bed this morning. The apartment wasn't big, a large room with an efficiency kitchen and eating area off to one corner, two closets and a bathroom. But the small space had a lot of character with high ceilings, crown molding, picture rails, tall wood pane windows and hardwood floors.

"It works well for what I need," she said. "It's in a safe area and reasonably priced."

He handed her the envelope. "Here you go."

"Thanks." She still couldn't believe Adam was here. "But you shouldn't have gone to so much trouble delivering it in person. I'll be at the lot tomorrow."

"I don't have a lot going on today."

A guy like him? She found that hard to believe. "I appreciate it."

"You weren't at the bar Friday night."

Megan hadn't thought a big-name star like him would hang out with the crew. "I was tired."

He slanted a brow. "Nothing else going on?"

"What do you mean?"

"Rob."

Oh, man. She wanted to die of embarrassment. "I haven't been throwing myself a pity party if that's what you're asking."

A sheepish grin formed on Adam's lips. "It was."

She grimaced. "I'm not a total loser. I was worn-out Friday night. The only thing I wanted to do was go home and crawl between the sheets."

Adam glanced at her queen-size bed with a brown-and-pink-striped comforter, light blue bed skirt and coordinating pillows on top. "Sounds like the perfect place to spend a Friday night."

His flirtatious, almost suggestive tone sounded warning bells in her head. She frowned. "It was. I slept. Alone."

Amusement danced in his eyes. "You look rested."

What was he doing here? She squared her shoulders. "I am."

"You were missed at the bar."

Yeah, right. No one ever missed her. Not when they hardly noticed when she was around. "That's nice of you to say, but I'm sure Kenna and Rosie were too busy flirting to notice I wasn't there."

"I wasn't talking about them," he clarified. "I missed you."

She hadn't been expecting that. "Oh."

"I sent you a text that night, but never heard back."

"I silenced my phone when I went to bed. I didn't want to be woken up. I never turned the sound back on."

"It's good to see you're okay."

Realization dawned. "The autographed photo was your excuse to come over."

"I wanted to make sure you were okay."

She didn't know if she should be annoyed or pleased. "I'm not some mentally unstable, psycho chick who would hurt myself."

"I know that."

"Then why are you here?"

He shifted his weight between his feet. "I remember how

upset my mom got when things didn't work out with a guy she liked."

"Pity party?"

"To the nth degree," he admitted. "She would stay in bed for days and cry her eyes out. If I hadn't brought her food, she wouldn't have eaten."

Sympathy replaced Megan's irritation. "Who took care of you while this was going on?"

He raised his chin. "I took care of myself."

Megan couldn't imagine. The only person she'd ever taken care of was her nephew, Brady, when she babysat. "How old were you?"

Adam walked farther into her studio. "It started when I was four. She can still be like that, but now she has a household staff to take care of her when it happens."

She knew the hardships Jess and Brady had been through. Adam might look like the golden boy, but his childhood sounded like it had been rough.

Megan touched his arm. His muscles tensed beneath her palm. "Adam…"

He shrugged off her hand. "It's nothing. Really."

His words didn't match the emotion darkening the color of his eyes. But he'd come over here out of concern for her. No way would she push or pry into something he didn't want to talk about.

"Well, you'll be relieved to know that not only have I not had a pity party, I also haven't shed one tear all weekend."

Which, come to think of it, was really weird. She had cried over Rob for much less over the years. Those sobfests used up boxes of tissue.

Why hadn't she cried this time?

Adam stared into her eyes. "Your eyes are clear and bright, not red and swollen."

She smiled smugly.

His gaze raked over her. "But you're still wearing pajamas."

Heat stole up Megan's neck until her cheeks burned. She'd

been so busy working on the sundress design she hadn't show-ered and changed. She glanced down. Bare feet. Purple zebra-striped fuzzy pants. A black camisole. No bra.

Oops. She crossed her arms over her chest, holding the en-velope in front of her like a shield. As if that would make a difference now...

His eyes, no longer dark, twinkled with mischief. "Don't be embarrassed. You look cute in your jammies."

Cute. The word sent a shiver down her spine.

Guys called their female friends cute. Women, at least those that men wanted to date, were labeled sexy. Not that she wanted to date Adam. She didn't. But she was wearing a cami with-out a bra.

And then she realized what was going on. Adam wasn't impressed with her average body. Why would he be when he was surrounded by knockouts like Lane Gregory's on a daily basis? Megan bit the inside of her cheek.

"No worries," he added. "Women go out in public wear-ing a lot less."

She remembered the women at the beach when she'd first met Adam. Those tiny bikinis barely covered anything. If he didn't think her body wasn't a big deal, she wasn't going to act embarrassed wearing her jammies and being braless in front of him. She uncrossed and lowered her arms.

"Check the picture," he said. "Make sure it's what you wanted."

"You mean what Rob wanted," she corrected.

Megan opened the envelope flap and removed an eight-by-ten glossy photograph. A gorgeous shot of him from an up-coming release, a movie, based on the watermark in the corner, titled *Navy SEALs*. She read his inscription.

Pru,
Happy Birthday! Thanks for being such a great fan.
Appreciate all your support.
Love,
Adam

"Thank you." His thoughtfulness warmed Megan's insides. "This will make Rob happy."

Adam's gaze met hers. "I want you to be happy."

Her heart skipped a beat. Maybe two. Okay, seven.

Looking down, she slid the photo back into the envelope. She placed the envelope on top of the table. "I am happy. I have my internship, this charming apartment and am making new friends on the set."

"So you've put Rob behind you?"

"He's with Prudence," Megan said. "Not much I can do about that."

"You could tell him how you feel."

Megan had lost her dad. She couldn't face the thought of losing Rob, too. That was a distinct possibility, more like a hundred percent probability, if she told him her true feelings. It was safer to plan and dream. "I can't."

Adam raised a brow. "Even if it means losing him to Prudence?"

The question swirled through Megan's mind. "I don't know."

"You might want to think about it." Adam strode to her chair where she'd been working on the sundress design. He set his sunglasses on an end table and picked up her sketchbook. "What's this?"

Megan inhaled sharply. "Nothing."

"It looks like something." He studied the page. "You drew this?"

Her muscles bunched. She'd never forgotten the way her mom laughed at Megan's first and only attempt to put on a fashion show. She should have known better, but she'd wanted her mother to be proud of her and tell people about both her daughters, not only Jess. "I was playing around this morning."

"You're talented."

What else was he going to say? *You suck?* "Thanks."

"Don't duck your head. I've been dragged to enough fashion weeks and costume meetings to know talent when I see it."

She straightened. "Design classes were my favorite in college. Nothing like putting on a piece of clothing that started with nothing more than a few lines on a sketchpad."

"This is for you?"

Maybe she'd been trying too hard to fit in. She raised her chin. "I might wear jeans at work, but that doesn't mean I wear them 24/7."

"You also wear pajamas."

"I should change."

"Not on my account."

Disappointment shot through her. "You're leaving."

"Not unless you want me to go."

"I don't." The words rushed out before she had time to think. "Unless you have somewhere else to go."

"I'd rather stay here," he said to her unexpected relief. "But I'm a casual type of guy so there's no need for you to put on something else. Pajamas are the perfect attire for a Sunday afternoon. I take it you were planning to take it easy today."

Megan fought the urge to cringe. She had asked Adam to stay. Here. With her. Maybe she needed her head examined, after all. "Um, yes. A little design work. Order a pizza. Watch a movie or two."

"Pizza and movies are two of my favorite things."

"O-kay." Her insides twisted with unease. "But you'd have more fun riding some wave or jumping off a building."

"This will be fun enough." He sat in her chair, crossing his feet at the ankles. "I'm not allowed to do any of my normal activities while we're shooting. Don't want to put the production in jeopardy."

"Thank you from someone grateful to have an internship during the shoot."

"You're welcome."

A beat passed. And another.

Megan didn't know what to say or do. Lying on a bed of knives might be more comfortable than this.

She didn't know if Adam was bored or lonely or simply a big flirt, but nothing like this had ever happened to her before with a guy other than Rob dropping by, much less a movie star. She wasn't sure how to handle it. Or him.

"So what kind of movie do you want to watch?" Adam asked. "A romantic comedy?"

"Straight comedy." Something romantic wouldn't be a smart idea with him here. Who was she kidding? Nothing about spending time with Adam was smart. In fact, she could be in real trouble if anyone in the costume department found out he was here. But she couldn't deny a part of her enjoyed the attention. She would have to be careful not to let that enjoyment go too far. "The cable has streaming videos on demand. You pick a movie. I'll order the pizza."

The thought of spending a Sunday afternoon relaxing had appealed to Adam on a gut level. He never hung out and did nothing. He was looking forward to it. Except being around Megan was far from relaxing.

Forget about watching the movie on the television, he wanted to look at her.

As if on cue Megan shifted positions on the bed, rolling onto her stomach. The scoop neck of her camisole gave him a better view of soft, ivory skin. His temperature shot up.

"This is a funny movie," she said.

Adam looked at the television screen. "Yeah."

His gaze wanted to stray back to her. It wasn't just her nice breasts or her expressive eyes, but the way her curly hair fell halfway down her back.

He was attracted. Very attracted.

That was bad. Very bad.

A perfectly good bed was going to waste at the moment, but he didn't care. Not when he felt as if he was struggling to remain in control around her. Not physically, though there was an element of that, but emotionally. Considering Adam didn't do emotion, he wasn't sure what to think.

She laughed at something from the movie.

He hadn't a clue what, but the sound curled around him like a lover's embrace.

What the hell was going on?

Okay, she was smart, funny, unpredictable, pretty, though she would disagree about that.

But none of those things explained why he lowered his guard around Megan. Something he never did. Worse, it didn't seem to be a conscious decision.

Maybe it was her honesty or her straightforwardness.

Maybe parts of Maxwell were seeping into Adam's real life.

But he couldn't believe he'd told her about his mom. No one, not even his agent, knew any of that. Adam hadn't even needed a lot of prompting.

Bad, bad, bad.

He didn't want anyone to know about his childhood and family. It was nobody's business and better left in the past.

Or forgotten altogether.

There was a reason he had flings not relationships. He'd learned the hard way that love only ended up hurting. It didn't last.

Which was why Megan should stay in the friend zone. Sure, he wanted to sleep with her. A friend with benefits. That might get her mind off Rob, but would that be the best thing for her? Adam's consideration of Megan's feelings was enough to tell him to stay far away from her. At least when it came to a physical relationship. He liked taking risks, but he wasn't stupid.

What if he really liked Megan? She was different enough she could turn his world inside out.

Not worth the risk.

Monday, Megan couldn't believe how the atmosphere on the set crackled with tension, a one-hundred-eighty-degree shift from Friday. Unforeseen delays had put a wrench into the schedule. Tempers flared. Voices rose. The background artists sat around with nothing to do except take up space.

An unexpected break gave Megan time to return Adam's

sunglasses. He'd forgotten them at her apartment yesterday. Passing them off in public rather than private would have been better. His friendliness and confidence appealed to her and sent her hormones into overdrive whenever he was near. But she hadn't seen him on the set.

At his trailer, Megan removed his sunglasses from her pocket. She'd cleaned the lenses last night and placed them in a padded holder so they wouldn't get damaged.

She had it all planned out—return the sunglasses, thank him for keeping her company yesterday and then say goodbye. No matter how much fun she had with him or how attractive he might be, keeping her distance was the smart thing to do.

This morning Eva had mentioned staying away from the lead actors. It was a generic warning, but a warning nonetheless. One that set warning bells ringing in Megan's head. A good thing Adam seemed satisfied with being friends. What guy spent an afternoon sitting on a bed and watching movies without making a move? Not one who was attracted to her. She must have her own spot reserved in the friend zone.

His trailer door was ajar.

Megan heard a voice, Adam's voice. He was rehearsing lines.

She waited at the door. He stopped talking. Something thudded. A book?

Megan knocked.

The door opened more from the weight of her hand against it.

"Not now," his harsh voice barked.

Megan felt like she'd been slapped, but she didn't think he knew it was her. She couldn't see him through the crack in the door. He doubted she could see him. "I have your sunglasses."

"Keep them."

She tried not to take his impatient tone personally. His moodiness was a total shift from how lighthearted he'd been yesterday. But she wasn't keeping his sunglasses. She wanted nothing to tie her to Adam, not even a little bit. For the sake of her internship, she rationalized. "I'll set them inside the door."

"Whatever."

As Megan opened the door farther, she saw Adam. He faced to the right side of the trailer, giving her a view of his profile.

Deep lines on his forehead and around his frowning mouth matched the tension in the air. He stared at the script in his hands. His grip tightened until an edge crinkled. With a shake of his head, he smoothed the wrinkles on the page with his thumb.

She hated how pained he seemed. But he'd made it clear he didn't want company. Time to get out of here. She set the sunglasses on a table.

As she backed out of the trailer, the door creaked.

He cursed. "Just go."

She hesitated. Adam looked like he needed a friend or a hug, but she doubted he'd admit it. "I'm going."

He glanced up from the script. "Megan?"

The emotion in his eyes filled her with compassion. His gaze, usually full of confidence and strength, contained a look she knew well—one of nerves and self-doubt.

Megan's heart melted at his unexpected vulnerability. "Sorry, I didn't mean to bother you. I wanted to return your sunglasses."

He dragged his hand through his hair, looking tortured. "Ignore me. I'm in a bad mood. The scene I'm shooting soon is killing me. I can't get the lines right."

She had no idea he took his acting so seriously. "I wish there was something I could do to help."

"There is." He handed her the script. "Read Calliope's part."

Maxwell's wife. Lane Gregory's role. Megan's stomach knotted. "O-kay, but I'm better dressing and undressing actors than being one."

Adam didn't crack a smile. He pointed to a line. "I'm going to start here. Ready?"

She nodded, even though she felt completely out of her element.

"Tell me the truth." He gazed deeply into Megan's eyes, making her insides quiver. "Are you involved in this?"

Megan glanced at the script. "Unbelievable. After everything we've been through…"

"Calliope."

His anguish, both visible and verbal, gave Megan goose bumps. "Max."

"Answer my question."

"You know my father. He thinks women are incapable of anything other than shopping and sex. He has never involved me in his business dealings. Legal or otherwise."

A beat passed. And another.

His nostrils flared. "Do you love me?"

His words sounded…mean. Spiteful. Wrong.

"Of course, I, um…" Her tongue stumbled over the next word. She lost her place in the script. "Sorry."

"It's not you," Adam said. "Those four words get me every time."

Do you love me?

A warm and fuzzy feeling flowed through her. She could fall in love with him.

Correction. Not Adam, Rob. She could fall in love with Rob.

Wait. She was already in love with Rob. At least she thought she was. She clutched the script.

"The emotion is off," Adam continued.

"You sounded mean, angry."

He blew out a puff of air. "I'm hitting the wrong notes. Maxwell wouldn't feel that way here. He's confused, trying to figure out what's going on and who set him up."

The frustration in Adam's voice tugged at Megan's heart. She wanted to help him. She'd never acted, but she'd spent plenty of time at the theater in college. She'd taken film courses because character and story could be enhanced by costumes. Surely all those hours hadn't been a waste of time and tuition.

She thought for a moment. "What do you want Calliope's answer to be? Not you, I mean, Maxwell."

Adam's brow furrowed. "I know what she says."

"So do I." Megan waved the script. "But is that the answer Maxwell wants to hear? Is he expecting her to say she doesn't or is he hoping she does? That might help you figure out the right emotion to use."

Adam closed his eyes. His lips moved, but no sound came out.

She stayed quiet so she wouldn't disturb him.

A minute, maybe two, passed. His eyes opened. The creases on his forehead remained, but they weren't as deep. The lines bracketing his mouth relaxed. "Let's try it again."

The dialogue flowed smoother this time. Megan still wasn't sure what she was doing, but knowing she was helping made her relax a little.

"You know my father. He thinks women are incapable of anything other than shopping and sex. He has never involved me in his business dealings. Legal or otherwise."

A beat passed. And another.

"Do you love me?" Anxiety gave an edge to the anticipation in his voice.

"Of course I love you." She sounded husky, unnatural.

"Prove it."

The potent mix of hope and fear in Adam's gaze mesmerized her. The line she was supposed to say flew from her mind. She glanced down at the script but the words had blurred.

Megan parted her lips, as if that would be enough of a prompt to make her remember what she was supposed to say.

"If you won't," he said. "I will."

Adam lowered his mouth to hers. His kiss jolted her. She gasped, but didn't back away.

Heat. Sparks. Proverbial fireworks.

His lips moved over hers with an expertise that left her breathless and wanting more. He touched her with only his mouth, but sensation pulsated through her until she curled her toes.

She arched against him, wanting to be closer to him. Her arms circled him. Her hands splayed his back.

The fireworks continued. The kissing, too.

She'd never been kissed like this, never felt this way before. She wanted it to keep going.

Slowly Adam ended the kiss and stepped back.

Her lips tingled. Her heart pounded.

Adam looked at her with a strange expression in his eyes, as if he were waiting for something.

Another kiss? Anticipation soared. "What?" she asked.

He blinked twice, then turned the script toward him. He ran his finger along the page, as if he'd lost his place, too, and pointed. "It's your line."

He sounded a little breathy. From the kiss? She hoped so because that was exactly how she sounded, too.

Megan focused on the words and reread. The script called for a passionate kiss between Calliope and Maxwell. Her heart dropped to her feet. The kiss hadn't been an impromptu one. It had followed one of the lines of dialogue.

Adam must have gotten caught up in the scene and kissed her, assuming she was going along with it, too.

Except she'd thought the kiss was for real. But while kissing him might have felt like the Fourth of July, the fireworks hadn't been real. This was a rehearsal for when he kissed another woman, a beautiful, sexy woman. Nothing more.

Instead of fueled by a mutual attraction and heat, the kiss had no real emotion to it. At least not from Adam. He flirted and was used to kissing women while acting. This wasn't about her or him but his career. That was where his vulnerability lay. If he truly had any interest in something deeper than friendship, he couldn't have kissed her so passionately, then stand there like it meant nothing.

But he *was* standing there as if nothing had happened between them.

Megan struggled to breathe. She needed to get away from him. Now.

"I need to get back to work." She handed him the script. "You don't need me anymore. You nailed the line."

His gaze remained on her. "Thanks for the help."

Megan didn't know how to reply because right now she was wishing she'd never stepped foot in his trailer. That kiss would stay with her a long time. Maybe forever.

"You're welcome," she said.

With that, Megan exited the trailer. She hurried back to the costume area. She touched her lips, still tingling and swollen. Losing herself in Adam's kiss had been a severe lapse of judgment, one she couldn't repeat. And wouldn't.

No matter how much she might want to kiss him again.

CHAPTER EIGHT

A THIRTYSOMETHING makeup artist named Basil patted Adam's forehead with a towel after the shoot had finally ended. The man beamed as bright as the silver earrings dangling from his earlobes. "You were simply amazing, Adam. If that kiss with Lane isn't nominated for an award, if it doesn't win, I'll eat a big fat beef burger."

He looked at Basil. "But you're a vegan."

Basil winked. "Exactly."

A satisfied feeling settled in the center of Adam's chest. The big emotional scene with Lane had gone off without a hitch. He wished he could take credit for his performance during all the takes this afternoon, but that belonged to one person—Megan. He'd gotten himself so worked up about flubbing his lines and making a fool of himself that he hadn't been able to think straight. She'd been a voice of reason, an angel saving him from embarrassment, a devil kissing him until the only thing he could think about was her. And more of her kisses.

Aware of Basil's gaze, Adam smiled. "Thanks. Appreciate your support."

Basil pulled the towel away with a flourish. Not surprising given the makeup artist's passion for flamenco dancing. "The pleasure is all mine."

Adam glanced around to see if Megan was on the set. Producers and invited guests sat in an area to the right of the set with cushy leather couches to lounge on and monitors to watch. The rest of the crew was either scattered among the cameras, lighting or other equipment.

No Megan.

He'd wanted her to see how well he did. He wanted to thank her. The way she'd kissed him this morning had rendered him speechless. He'd been turned on and uncertain at the same time. Not a good combination.

"You naughty boy," Lane whispered from behind him. "Not letting me know you kissed like that. I was hoping Damon needed another close-up."

Adam hadn't been thinking about Lane while kissing her. Calliope hadn't entered his head, either. Only Megan. She might seem like a forever type of girl, but she had kissed him back eagerly, almost recklessly. Maybe acting the part of Calliope had given her the chance to break free of whatever was holding her back and making her cling to her so-called plans. He had to wonder how reckless she might be willing to be with him.

"Just playing my part," he said.

"We should practice for our upcoming love scene." Lane blew softly in his ear, making him want to scratch the affected skin. "Your trailer or mine?"

The woman was relentless, even though her fiancé was somewhere on the set. "I told you my rules."

Lane frowned. "I thought you were a player."

Adam wasn't about to play with her. "You're in a league by yourself. I wouldn't want to try to compete there."

Confusion clouded her gaze.

This was his opportunity to go. "I need to change. So do you."

As Adam walked toward the dressing rooms, crew members gave him kudos and atta-boys for his work. Everyone said they couldn't wait to see the dailies. Neither could he. That acting nomination was getting so much closer Adam could taste it.

It took him over a half hour to reach the dressing room due

to receiving so many accolades. Rosie was waiting for him. Megan, too.

Today kept getting better and better. Adam smiled at the two women, but his gaze lingered on the intern.

Megan's cheeks were no longer flushed. Her lips didn't look as swollen from kissing him this morning. A lanyard with laminated pictures of actors in their costumes hung around her neck. Comparing a character to the picture gave the costume dressers a fast and easy way to determine continuity between takes. He kicked off his shoes. "Sorry it took me so long, ladies."

"No worries." Rosie placed his shoes into a labeled bag. "You earned every single one of those compliments. Great job."

"You were watching?"

Rosie nodded. "We all were."

Megan must have watched, too. That pleased him. But she wouldn't meet his eyes. Adam didn't know if that was because of their earlier kiss or the scenes he'd shot. He liked the idea she might be jealous of him kissing Lane all afternoon, but that was probably stretching things given her feelings for Rob, the engineering bozo with the supposedly high IQ.

"Thanks," Adam said.

"Texas has been enlisted to help today," Rosie explained. "Kenna was called in to assist with Lane, who's acting more like a spoiled brat than America's sweetheart."

His fault. Now the crew would have to put up with Lane being in a bad mood. He'd be buying the rounds on Friday night after Damon showed this week's dailies. Spending money on the crew was better than fooling around with Lane. "I'm sure you'll show Megan the ropes."

"Speaking of ropes." Rosie winked. "After seeing the way you kissed Lane, Texas might have to tie me up to keep me in line with you."

Adam's gaze met Megan's. "Promises, promises."

She blushed, turning her cheeks a pretty pink.

"Let's get you out of this costume," Rosie said.

A wicked idea formed in his head. Remembering the feel of Megan's lips on his, her sweet, warm taste, he wondered what it would be like to have her undress him. Adam flexed his fingers. "I have stuff on my hands. Would you mind?"

"I'll get a wet cloth," Megan offered.

"No, we've taken long enough. We still have to get ready for the close-up shot." Rosie removed his accessories, checking them off on her inventory list and placing them in Ziploc bags. She pinned that to the accessory holder, a muslin sleeve that was a foot to a foot and a half long. "Unbutton Adam's shirt for him."

Megan inhaled sharply.

He almost felt bad for her deer-in-the-headlights expression. Emphasis on *almost*. He planned to make the most of this unexpected opportunity.

Megan's fingers trembled as she reached for his shirt button.

Her nervousness tugged at his heart. "I don't bite."

"He doesn't." Rosie removed his watch and placed it in a Ziploc plastic bag. "Adam's more a nibbler."

"You know this how?" he asked jokingly.

Rosie grinned. "I have my sources."

"Sources that are wrong," he countered.

Megan's fingers fumbled. She finally unfastened one, but she wasn't smiling.

Maybe this hadn't been such a good idea.

"So you're a biter, then?" Rosie teased.

Megan's fingers slipped off the next button. Her fingertips brushed his chest. Heat pooled where she touched him.

Some strong physical attraction...chemistry there. But he'd known that from their kiss.

Her flushed cheeks deepened from pink to red. "Sorry."

"I'm sorry. I should have had Basil deal with my hands before coming here." Adam wanted her to laugh, not be nervous and tense. "You're doing great."

Rosie's phone beeped. She checked the touch screen, then grimaced. "I'll be right back."

With that, she dashed out of the dressing room.

Megan's hands froze. "Your hands are fine. Basil took care of them, didn't he?"

Adam smiled sheepishly. "I knew you were a sharp one."

She placed her arms at her sides. "Hurry up and unbutton your shirt before Rosie gets back. Pants, too. I'm not unzipping your zipper."

Adam would have loved her to unzip him, but he'd given Megan enough grief. He did as she'd asked.

She readied a hanger for his shirt. "You and Lane were great today. You, especially. I didn't think you could be any better than you were this morning. I was wrong."

Others' compliments paled in comparison to hers. "I was hoping you were there."

"I wanted to be there," Megan admitted. "But I didn't realize there would be so many takes for one kiss."

He handed her his shirt. "They have to get all the angles."

"Well, it gave me plenty of opportunity to see how you acted out the scene with Lane compared to the one with me."

"It was the same."

"During the main takes, you kissed Lane longer."

Interesting, Megan had noticed that. Maybe he shouldn't have downplayed the kiss in the trailer. But her rock-his-world kiss had caught him off guard. Self-preservation had made him act as if the kiss had been nothing when it had been something. Something big. "Not intentional."

She stared down her nose at him. "None of my concern if it was."

The lines around her mouth and tight voice begged to differ. He wondered if that meant she wasn't so dead set on the guy back in Texas in spite of what she'd said. "I was taking Damon's request to make the moment more emotional, but I wasn't timing any of the kisses."

She lifted her chin. "I didn't time the kisses, either. But the ones with Lane were definitely longer."

Satisfaction flowed through him. Megan was jealous.

"That's only because every time I kissed Lane I imagined I was kissing you."

Excitement flashed in Megan's eyes, but quickly disappeared. "Yeah, right."

"I'm not joking." He glanced at the closed door to the dressing room and lowered his voice. "Just so you know, you're a much better kisser than Lane Gregory."

Gratitude shone in Megan's stunning brown eyes. "If I wasn't afraid of someone walking in or the fact I decided not to kiss you again, I'd plant a big fat one right on your lips for saying that. Whether it's true or not."

"Trust me, it's true." He liked her sassy response, but he hated how she didn't see herself as desirable. He wanted to kiss all the uncertainty out of her. "But why don't you want to kiss me?"

"Other than the fact that you're the star and could have me fired quicker than snapping your fingers?"

Her words stung. "I would never do anything to hurt you or get you fired."

She buttoned his shirt. "You say that now, but you could change your mind."

"I'm not like that."

She placed the hanger on a clothing rack. "No, I don't think you are."

Her words didn't make him feel much better. He unbuckled his belt. "What else?"

As she faced him, he unzipped his pants.

She gasped, covered her eyes with her hands and turned away from him. "What are you doing?"

"Taking off my pants."

Megan kept her back to him. "I thought you'd go into the bathroom or something."

"Why would I do that?" He didn't understand why she was so upset. "This is a dressing room."

"But I'm here."

"Come on. It's not like we're twelve."

She didn't say anything.

Adam supposed she might not be used to the lack of modesty. "I'm sorry if I surprised you, but actors dress and undress in front of people all the time. I don't think twice before stripping down to my underwear."

She lowered her hands from her eyes, but didn't turn around. "Are you wearing underwear?"

A little prudish, but still cute. "Do I look like the commando type?"

"Must I answer?"

He smiled. "I'm wearing boxer briefs. Fully covered. Satisfied?"

"Take off your pants and hand them to me." Megan didn't look at him, but reached behind her. "I'll hang them up."

"Turn around. If you're going to be in costume design, you can't get all wigged out by a guy undressing in front of you." He slipped out of his pants, but didn't hand them to her. "It's not like you haven't seen a naked man before."

Glancing over her shoulder, she met his gaze. "I haven't. At least not in person. Unless you count sculptures in museums."

He stared at her in disbelief. No way could she be...

"Please don't look at me like that," she pleaded. "I might not have slept with anyone, but that doesn't mean I have some sort of incurable disease or a giant *V* on my chest.

V for virgin. His throat tightened. "Most women your age have had sex."

Her eyes darkened. "I'm not like most women."

No, she wasn't.

Squaring her shoulders as if she were facing a troop of armed soldiers rather than a guy in his underwear, Megan faced him. She kept her gaze focused on his face. "Give me your pants."

He handed them to her. "Does Rob know?"

"I have no idea." She zipped the pants. "He knows I haven't dated much."

"You've been saving yourself for him."

She cringed. "That sounds so…pathetic."

"It's sweet and romantic."

Like her.

She buckled his belt. "If the crew finds out, they'll think I'm a freak or frigid or something."

"Having sex while working on a shoot happens, but not everyone is doing it."

He wasn't. That would surprise the crew more than Megan being a virgin. But he wasn't going to tell her that.

"Maybe Rob knows and that's why he doesn't want me." The hurt and embarrassment in her voice made Adam's stomach hurt. "Because I'm inexperienced."

"If that's the case, Rob is not only an idiot, but also a total moron."

"I suppose giving it up to the first guy I see would be pretty stupid."

Not if she were giving it up to him. He was the guy she was looking at. Introducing Megan to sex would be fun. He would be better doing that for her than someone as clueless as Rob.

"I mean I know what my sister has gone through being a single mom." Megan hung up the pants. "That's a road I don't want to follow."

"Having sex doesn't mean you'll automatically get pregnant."

She removed his wedding band and placed it in the plastic bag with his watch. "Not having sex guarantees I won't."

"I'll concede that point." Adam might want her, but he wanted it to be the right choice for her. "You shouldn't just give it up. The first time is a big deal. Or it should be."

There. He'd said what needed to be said, told her good advice and provided the necessary support. If this were a romantic comedy, he would have given the perfect best friend performance. Now he wouldn't have to feel guilty when he took her to bed.

Oh, the things he could teach her. Playful images filled his mind.

"That's the real reason I've waited," she said. "I want my first time to be with someone I love and trust and who feels the same way about me."

Damn. That didn't describe Adam at all.

Talk about a bummer. But maybe this was for the best.

Someone with a big heart like Megan would never treat sex as simply a physical act of gratification. She would become attached and want a relationship and other things Adam wasn't willing to give. She deserved all those things. He wanted her to have them. Best to curtail his flirting with her.

"Wait for that right guy." Adam couldn't believe the words had come out of his mouth, but he kept going as if some alien being had taken residency in his body, especially his heart, and pushed out any thought of selfishness. "Having sex isn't something you do to fit in. Don't let anyone push you into doing something until it's the way you want it to be."

Her smile brightened her entire face. It was as if the sun had appeared after being covered by clouds. Simply beautiful. Breathtaking.

"Thank you. I don't feel like such a freak now," she said. "You're really something, Adam Noble. Just when I think you can't get any nicer, you do."

His heart slammed against his chest. He struggled to fill his lungs with air. What was happening?

Megan wasn't the anomaly. He was.

If any of his friends had heard him, they'd confiscate his player status, delete all the hot chicks' phone numbers from his contact list and laugh him right out of town. Adam swallowed. "Just don't let anybody know."

The V above her nose deepened again. "About being a virgin?"

"That I can be such a nice guy." His jaw tensed. "I'm a leading man, not a best friend. You'd be wise to remember that."

He'd spoken the words for his sake as much as hers. Unfortunately, Adam had a feeling he might be the one struggling not to forget them.

* * *

Hurry up and wait. That seemed to be how things worked on the set. The days ran into one another, one week into the next. Megan had finally gotten into the swing of things, but she never knew exactly what she would be doing each day when she arrived at the lot.

The only problem, if she could call it a problem, was Adam. Megan thought they were friends, but she no longer saw him except at meal times or if she went onto the set to watch a scene being shot. If she didn't know better she would think he was avoiding her.

Maybe he was.

I'm a leading man, not a best friend. You'd be wise to remember that.

Did he mean he wasn't a friend type or her friend? Not knowing frustrated her. But what could she do about it? She wasn't supposed to be hanging around him. She couldn't force him to be her friend or spend time with her or make him kiss her again.

Strike the kisses. More of those were bad ideas.

But she missed her conversations with him, his smile, his sense of humor.

Tuesday evening, Megan followed Kenna and Rosie out of the wardrobe department. The two women had taken Megan under their wing, both professionally and personally. Even though they were older than her, they didn't seem to mind her being younger and new to the set. She enjoyed working with them and hanging out during meal times and breaks, talking about work, fashion, men. It was the kind of relationship she had always wanted with her sister. The kind of relationship Jess had had with their mother. But Megan hadn't told them, or anyone, about kissing Adam while they rehearsed lines. She wanted to keep that secret. Her secret.

An outdoor scene was being shot tonight so call times had been shifted later. Everyone would eat dinner, then prepare for the shoot.

Kenna rubbed her hands together. "I hope there's salmon."

"Beef brisket and corn bread would be nice," Megan said.

"Homesick, Tex?" Rosie asked.

"No." Megan hadn't heard from her family. Not that she'd thought about them much the past few days. Rob, either. That was odd. Guess she was busier than she realized. "But I'm hungry."

Whatever they were serving for dinner smelled delicious.

Craft Services provided all the snacks and drinks the crew could want, but a caterer, in this case a Cordon Bleu–trained chef, prepared meals. The food was to die for. Tasty, healthy and priced right—free. Megan was on her feet so much, working crazy hours, she was losing weight in spite of food being available all the time.

"You know what they say." Rosie picked up a plate. "A well-fed crew helps a production run smoother."

"Let's hope that's true tonight," Kenna said in a low voice. "Rumor has it there are lighting 'issues.'"

Rosie sighed. "I hope not. I don't want to be here all night."

"Tony had an early call time," Kenna said of her gaffer boyfriend who she met on the set. "He hinted things weren't going well."

Delays happened for a variety of reasons—equipment breaking, weather for outdoor shoots, props and lighting. Some setups, especially exterior scenes, could be complicated and take hours.

Megan stood behind her two friends in the line for dinner. "A good thing we could sleep in this morning."

"I needed the rest," Rosie said.

Megan picked up a plate. "Me, too."

Waking without an alarm had been so great. Dreaming about Adam Noble, not so much. She needed to get him out of her thoughts once and for all. He hadn't even placed her in friend zone. He didn't want to be her friend.

Better that way, she kept telling herself. Maybe one of these times the words would sink in and not bother her so much.

Megan went through the buffet. The delicious aromas made

her mouth water. No brisket, but she helped herself to a generous helping of pulled pork, steamed green beans, a baked sweet potato with butter and brown sugar and a glass of iced tea. She joined Rosie and Kenna at a table.

"Where's your dessert?" Rosie asked.

Megan placed a napkin on her lap. "I'll get a brownie later."

As they ate, they discussed fashion trends for the fall. The topic turned to an upcoming awards show.

Kenna scooped up another forkful of salmon. "I can't wait to see what people will be wearing at the Viewers' Choice Awards."

Rosie nodded. "I love seeing all those gowns on the red carpet no matter what the awards show."

"There are so many of them. They all start sounding the same," Megan admitted.

Kenna nodded, and started ticking award ceremonies off on her fingers with exaggerated yawns. Midlaughter, Megan realized Adam stood next to their table with a plate of food in one hand and a glass of water in the other.

"Mind if I join you?" Adam asked,

Megan's heart bumped. She opened her mouth to speak, but nothing came out. He gave new meaning to the term "smart casual" in his cerulean polo shirt and khaki pants. The shirt intensified the green in his eyes. Her pulse accelerated.

Stop staring.

She glanced at the other two women, who motioned for Adam to sit.

Adam took a step toward the empty chair next to her, much to Megan's delight. Maybe he wasn't ignoring her, after all. But then he changed direction to her dismay. He pulled out the chair next to Kenna on the opposite side of the table from Megan and sat. "Thanks."

Disappointment tugged at her. Too bad she hadn't picked up a brownie. Chocolate sounded good right now. Megan stabbed her fork into her sweet potato and took a bite. Brown sugar and butter didn't have the same emotional benefits as a chunk of chocolate.

Adam stared across the table at her. "Do you like awards shows?"

"I've watched them on TV," Megan said.

"What you see on TV is staged," Kenna said. "The real fun is when the red light on the camera goes off. The emcee tells funnier jokes."

Rosie nodded. "And the seat fillers run around in their gowns and tuxes while someone races to the bathroom."

Adam placed his cup on the table. "I did that."

"Race to the bathroom?" Megan asked.

"Sit in empty seats during breaks," he said.

Kenna's mouth formed a perfect O. "I had no idea."

Adam shrugged. "It was a paying gig. One where I didn't have to fall out of a building or roll across the top of a car."

Rosie smiled. "Lucky you. I don't have that kind of claim to fame, but I have been enlisted to make impromptu fashion repairs in the ladies' powder room as well as tape breasts to ensure no nip slips."

Adam winked. "That sounds like a better gig than mine."

The man was incorrigible. A total flirt. And absolutely gorgeous. Megan stared at the food on her plate, but nothing looked appetizing any longer.

"I've only attended some after-parties," Kenna said.

Rosie stared over her cola can. "Those are much better than the awards show."

"Why is that?" Megan asked.

Rosie grinned. "Drinking, dancing, more drinking."

Kenna looked at Megan. "We should try to get invites for a party after the Viewers' Choice Awards so Tex can see what it's like."

Megan's first instinct was to decline. She'd never been into parties, but then again, she'd never been invited to many. "That would be fun."

Adam's mouth quirked. "You'd want to go?"

She thought for a moment. Dancing sounded fun. "Yes, I would."

Rosie batted her eyelashes at Adam. "Maybe some hot actor nominated for favorite onscreen couple could get our names on some after-party lists."

He squinted. "What's wrong with your eyes?"

Rosie punched his shoulder. "You're worse than my brother."

Adam laughed. "I take that as a compliment. I'll see what I can do about getting you ladies on a couple of lists."

"Thanks." Kenna rubbed her hands together. "That gives us two weeks to plan our outfits. Think you can do it?"

Megan nodded. She wondered if Adam would be at the same party. Not that it mattered.

"We'll need at least a week to figure out what shoes to wear," Rosie said. "Though I'm sure we'll be barefoot by night's end from all the dancing."

"You mean when the sun comes up," Kenna said.

Adam grinned at the redhead. "I like how you think."

Picking up her iced tea, Megan wondered if he knew Kenna was dating Tony. Not that who Adam flirted with or liked was any of Megan's business. For all she knew, he'd hooked up with someone on the set and that was why he hadn't been around. She wasn't thirsty, but she sipped her tea to give herself something to do other than think about him.

"You're the planner," Adam said to her. "Anything your partners in crime are forgetting for your big night?"

Megan set her glass on the table. Invite, dress, shoes... "Hair and makeup."

"Basil!" Kenna and Rosie said at the same time.

Adam grinned. "Looks like you're all set."

"All set for what?" Eva asked, standing next to the table.

CHAPTER NINE

THE appearance of Firebreather cast a pall over the table. Conversation screeched to a halt. Excitement died.

Kenna and Rosie stared at their plates. Megan, too. She wanted to avoid making eye contact with their boss, if only to keep from being sent on an errand.

"All set for their night on the town," Adam said, rather bravely, Megan thought.

Eva arched a brow. "With you?"

Kenna looked up. "We know better than that."

Rosie nodded. Megan, too.

"So you've explained my rule to the intern," Eva said.

It wasn't a question.

"I heard about it, too." Adam's jaw tensed. "Not that they have anything to worry about from me."

Eva's hard gaze didn't waver from Adam's. "Did you know Lane had Annie Rockwell fired because her fiancé made a passing comment about how attractive the woman was?"

Megan hadn't heard that. But she knew who Annie was. The pretty assistant camerawoman had a Zumba-instructor-worthy body.

"I'm not like that," Adam said through clenched teeth.

"Maybe not," Eva agreed. "But better safe than sorry. These three women are important, talented members of my team."

Important? Talented? That was the first compliment Eva had ever given Megan. Pride flowed through her.

"I'd hate to lose any of them due to an…indiscretion," Eva continued. "And finding a replacement in the middle of a production would be a real pain."

"No worries." Adam cracked a smile. "We're all friends here. Just friends."

He hadn't been treating Megan like a friend lately. More like an acquaintance, a not so fond one, or a stranger.

"You can't have too many friends." Eva looked around the table until her gaze came to rest on Megan, who shifted in her chair under the watchful stare. "The shoot has been delayed two hours. Be back before nine."

With that, Eva walked away, but kept glancing back.

"Firebreather is on the warpath," Rosie mumbled.

Nodding, Kenna stood. "I want to go find Tony."

"Have fun," Megan said. "This is my chance to check out some of the other sets on the lot."

"I'll see you ladies, later." Adam stood. "I'm off to sound-stage three to say hi to my agent."

Rosie stood. "Maybe you could get Texas headed in the right direction so she doesn't get lost?"

Spending time with Adam appealed to Megan, but not this way. She didn't want him to feel obligated to be with her. "Thanks, Rosie, but I drove all the way from Texas on my own. I'm sure I can figure out which way to go."

"We don't want Rosie to worry," Adam said. "I'm happy to show you the way."

Megan leaned back in her chair. This wasn't what she wanted. Adam, either. He wouldn't have offered to escort her without the prompting from Rosie. Hurt pricked at Megan. She would prefer him to *want* to be with her. Not be so much like…

Rob.

The realization took Megan's breath away. Her insides twisted. No way did she want another situation like that in her life. Once was bad enough.

Time to grab a brownie or two and find something else to do. No, Megan realized. That would be stupid. She wanted to see the lot, and she would. But she didn't need Adam pointing her in the right direction. She could find her own way.

Adam was alone at the table with Megan, but didn't dare sit again. Not when he felt like a moth to her flame. He'd been trying to stay away from her. Not flirt. He should have eaten dinner in his trailer.

Except, he'd missed her. Like Rosie, he didn't want her wandering off and getting lost. "Ready?"

Megan rose and walked to the garbage can with her plate and cup.

What the... He did a double take.

She wasn't wearing jeans. He'd noticed she was wearing a button-up shirt with a lace-trimmed camisole underneath when she was sitting, but now that she stood he could see her complete outfit...

He blew out a puff of air.

The stylish tunic and leggings showed off her long legs and accentuated the curve of her hips and narrow waist. She'd exchanged her sneakers for a pair of leather flats. Pretty. Fashionable. Hot.

He followed after her. "New clothes."

She nodded. "I went shopping."

"You look great." He'd wondered what she had done on her time off. Not that he'd been thinking about her 24/7. Okay, maybe he had. "You must have had fun shopping with Kenna and Rosie."

Megan raised her chin. "I didn't go with them."

Her reply surprised Adam. Unless Kenna was with Tony the gaffer, the three women hung out during breaks. "Did you go shopping on your own?"

Her nose scrunched. "Huh?"

"Never mind," he said. "Let's go."

"Thanks for telling Rosie you'd get me going in the right direction," Megan said. "But I have a map. I'll be fine on my own."

No way. For some unexplained reason, Megan brought out his protective instinct. Must be some leftover character stuff from that SEAL commando he'd played. But Adam couldn't deny he liked being with her, too. Even if it went against his better judgment. "I'm going that way. It's no problem."

She stared at him.

He stared back.

Stalemate.

"Okay," she said finally, sounding annoyed. That bothered Adam. He'd hardly seen her. He would have thought she would want to spend time with him.

Megan walked alongside him in silence.

"How are things going?" he asked.

"Well." She looked at each of the buildings they passed, as if they were more interesting than him. "How about you?"

"No complaints." At least he'd had none until now. They'd never lacked for subjects to discuss. "Is something wrong?"

"No."

"You're quiet."

She shot him a sideways glance. "I didn't think you wanted to talk to me."

"Why would you think that?" he asked.

"You've been avoiding me since that night in your dressing room."

Damn. She'd nailed it. He hedged. "We've both been busy with the shoot."

Her gaze met his. "I made you uncomfortable."

Hell, yes. She made him uncomfortable. Not only then, but now. The scent of her shampoo filled his nostrils. He remembered the taste of her lips.

What was going on? Adam brushed his hand through his hair.

"You don't have to answer. It's pretty clear I do." She stopped at an intersection. "This is where we part ways."

He wasn't ready to say goodbye. "I'll go with you."

"Soundstage three is the other way."

The hurt arcing through him caught Adam by surprise. "You don't want me to go with you."

She set her jaw. "No."

Her firm tone dug into him, as did her answer. "Why not?"

"The truth?"

He nodded once, bracing himself for what she might say.

Hurt clouded her eyes. "I thought we were friends."

He tried to understand where she was going with this. Tried and failed. "We are."

"Your actions imply otherwise."

Once again she'd called him on his bad behavior. Okay, he had been acting like a jerk. But being with her confused him. He wasn't sure what to do or say. Avoiding her meant he didn't have to deal with the uncertainty, something that reminded him too much of his childhood. "I'm a guy. I don't put a lot of thought into what I'm doing or saying."

"Sounds like most men."

Rob? No, Adam didn't want to go there. He wanted Megan thinking about him. "Would it help if I apologized?"

"Only if you mean it."

"I do," he admitted. "I'm sorry for acting like a jerk. Again. I'd promise not to do again, but I'm a guy so who knows what will happen?"

A smile tugged on her lips. "At least you're honest."

"I am." He grinned. "And so are you. You don't hold back what you are thinking or feeling."

That familiar V above her nose returned. "With you, no."

He wanted to see a big smile back on her face. "Hey. Before you head off on your own, let me show you one thing."

"Your agent…"

"Sam can wait," Adam said. "Please."

She looked off into the distance, not really focusing on anything. But she wasn't zoning out. She was…thinking, no doubt performing a pro/con analysis to his offer.

"One thing," she said finally.

Relief washed over him. He took her hand.

She stiffened, but didn't pull her arm away. "What are you doing?"

"Showing you something."

Holding her hand, he led her across the street and through the alley of two buildings. This part of the lot was empty except for a helicopter flying overhead.

A few minutes later, anticipation revved through him. Adam hoped she liked this. He released her hand and covered her eyes.

She tensed. "What is going on?"

"Hold on." He coaxed her forward around the corner. "I want this to be a surprise."

"I'm not big on surprises," she said, sounding irritated.

"Trust me. You'll like this one. Keep your eyes closed." He positioned her in the middle of the street and removed his hand. "You can look now."

Megan opened her eyes and gasped. "It's New York."

They stood in a replica of Times Square, complete with large video screens and neon lights. He motioned to the street with both hands. "Welcome to the Big Apple."

Excitement filled her eyes. She spun around. "The set looks so real."

The same awe filled her voice as the first time they'd walked through the lot together. He was happy she hadn't lost that sense of wonder after being on the set. "Movie magic."

Her mouth slanted. "Or a talented group of set designers and carpenters."

Adam grinned. Practical. That was his Megan.

Not his, he corrected. Well, his friend.

"It's amazing," she said. "I've never been to New York, but I feel like I've been there now."

"Never been to New York with your interest in costume design and fashion?"

"Nope. I've always wanted to go. Experience the city that never sleeps. Get a taste of some glitz and glamour." She touched the brick facade of one of the buildings. "But I…"

As her voice faded, sadness filled her eyes.

He touched her shoulder. "What?"

"It's nothing."

"It's something." Adam gave her a reassuring squeeze. "I understand if you're still angry at me for the way I've been acting, but I am your friend and I'd like to know what's going on."

Megan took a breath. And another. "My mom never wanted any of us to go to New York. I finally realized why after my sister found an unopened letter hidden beneath my mother's jewelry box. It was written by my dad's first wife, Fenella. The return address on the envelope was New York City."

"The rancher and a city girl."

"Yep. I'm assuming my mom didn't want my dad anywhere near his first wife. Nor any of us." Megan peered in the window of a storefront. "Fenella was pregnant with twins when they divorced. I have a half brother and sister that I never knew about."

"That had to be a shock."

Megan nodded with a pained expression. "It's been a little weird."

Adam guessed more than a little. Losing her dad, finding out about new siblings. Megan had been through a lot in the past year. "Have you met them?"

"No, but one, Ellie, is now living in Larkville," Megan said. "I didn't have time to go home before leaving college for L.A. so I haven't met her. I'm glad to be here and not have to deal with it. Is that bad?"

Adam gave her a half hug. "Sounds smart to me."

She glanced up at him. "Thanks."

"Anytime." Something seemed to draw them closer. A part of Adam liked the feeling, but another part of him wanted to get the hell out of Dodge. "I have no idea what my father's life was like before or after us. I've always wondered if I had any secret half siblings."

"Is there any way to find out?" she asked.

"I hired a private detective, but he couldn't find any trace of my father. He told me Noble most likely wasn't my father's real name."

Megan gave Adam a squeeze.

The gesture, her warmth, comforted him. This time he wasn't about to shrug it off. Or her.

"My father was a con man. A charming liar. If he kept the same M.O. and moved on to another town and woman, I could have half siblings all over the place." Adam gazed down at her. So pretty. Compassion gleamed in her eyes. "We're a pair, aren't we?"

She nodded once. The light from the streetlamp made her lips glimmer. "But we're very different, too. Small-town girl and a famous movie star."

Adam didn't care about their differences. He wanted to kiss her. Badly. He could if he wanted to. The set was deserted except for the two of them. Silent except for their breaths. No one would have to know.

Megan parted her lips, a sign she wanted a kiss.

All he had to do was lower his head a couple of inches, to capture her lips with his. He knew how she would taste and feel.

His pulse quickened.

But something held him back.

I want my first time to be with someone I love and trust and who feels the same way about me.

A kiss was a long way from having sex, but he couldn't forget what she'd told him. He liked Megan, more than he'd liked anybody in a long time. Maybe ever. But he knew better than to love and trust anybody. Going down that path only led to heartache and disappointment. Places he had no intention of going. Watching his mother experience it over and over again was enough.

Gold flecks flamed in Megan's eyes.

He wanted to kiss her, but he wouldn't. Not until he explained what he was willing to give and what he couldn't. As soon as he figured out what that would be. Until then, he'd better stop thinking about her that way. "You'll get a taste of the movie star life at the after-parties."

"I can't wait to see all the dresses in person."

Her excitement pleased him. He wasn't that surprised she was more interested in the fashion than the stars wearing them. "You should be at the red carpet."

"That would be so cool," she admitted. "But attending an after-party is more than I imagined I'd do out here. I'm happy with that."

The hint of wistfulness in her voice stirred something within him. She might be content going to the after-party, but he felt the urge to do something more for her, to make her forget all she'd been through these past months with her family.

Megan had never been to New York. Larkville didn't sound like the most happening place. But he could give her a taste of the glitz and glamour she wanted to experience. More than she'd get attending an after-party. "Go with me to the Viewers' Choice Awards."

She let go of his arm. "What?"

"I want to take you to the awards show. You can experience one of Hollywood's big nights from start to finish," he said. "Rosie and Kenna can meet us at one of the after-parties."

"I...I don't know."

"What's not to know? Awards show, after-parties, a handsome escort."

"I appreciate the offer, but—"

"No buts," he interrupted. "All you have to do is say yes and you'll get to walk down the red carpet with me at your side."

That got her attention. Anticipation sparkled her eyes.

"Imagine seeing all those gowns up close and personal."

She moistened her lips. "That would be...nice."

"Not nice. Awesome," he countered. "I promise you'll have a great time."

"I'd really love to go." Concern clouded her gaze. "Except I...can't."

He hoped this had nothing to do with Rob. "Why not?"

"Eva. If she found out…"

Not Rob. Adam smiled. "Don't worry. I'll take care of Eva and any concerns she might have about you and me being… friends."

Megan threw her arms around him and hugged him tightly. "Thanks."

He hugged her back, inhaling her sweet scent. She felt so good in his arms. Sweet torture. "Thank you."

Megan felt as if she floated through the rest of the evening. Not even the lighting delays could bring her down. She couldn't believe Adam had invited her to the awards show, especially when he was up for an award. She wanted to tell Kenna and Rosie, but not until he'd had a chance to talk to Eva about it.

The only thing that would have made things better was if Adam had kissed her. She thought he might until she realized he saw her as only a friend. The way she wanted him to see her, Megan reminded herself. She shouldn't complain about that.

Except his invitation made her wonder if more than friend-ship was…possible.

The next day, she double-checked the racks of clothing for the background artists. Excitement had kept her awake most of the night. She still felt as if she were floating.

"So Adam Noble invited you to the Viewers' Choice Awards."

The sound of Eva's voice made Megan spin around. She held a clipboard in front of her chest and took a steadying breath. "I hope that's okay."

Eva pursed her red-glossed lips. "Are you sleeping with him?"

"No." Megan's voice came out sharper than she intended, but she hadn't held on to her virginity this long to give it up to the first gorgeous guy who'd paid attention to her. No matter how tempting. "We're…friends."

Friends who had shared kisses in his trailer hot enough to melt the rubber soles of Megan's tennis shoes and had her dreaming of more kisses, but Eva didn't need to know that. Especially since no more kisses had followed. And wouldn't.

Friends, Megan reminded herself. She wasn't ready to take that plunge into something more.

Eva studied Megan's face. "He said the same thing. That you were just friends."

Disappointment bounced down to Megan's feet and back up again. Maybe she was more ready than she realized. No, she needed be smart about this. Her internship came first. Not romance with a guy who'd told her and her boss they were just friends. She tilted her chin. "It's true."

"I didn't believe him, but I believe you."

Megan blushed. "May I go with Adam?"

"If I say no?"

"I won't go. This internship is more important than attending an awards show."

"Good answer."

Eva wasn't going to allow it. Megan's shoulders sagged.

"Stand up straight," Eva snapped. "You can't have bad posture when you're on the red carpet."

Megan straightened. Excitement stirred beneath her chest. "I can go?"

Eva narrowed her blue eyes. "Yes, but you'd better not do anything to make me regret this."

"I won't. I promise. On my father's grave." Megan wanted to hug Eva, but thought better of it. "Thank you."

Eva's assessing gaze traveled the length of Megan. No doubt assembling an inventory of all the things wrong with her. It would be a long list.

She fought the urge to squirm. She wouldn't give Firebreather the satisfaction.

"The Viewers' Choice Awards is a formal event," Eva said finally. "Do you have anything appropriate to wear? Shoes? Accessories?"

Her boss's critical tone bristled. "I have a dress."

"Off the rack?"

Megan raised her chin. "I made it."

"For a class?"

"For me."

Surprise flashed in Eva's eyes, but vanished as quickly as it had appeared.

The dress was one she'd mentioned to Rob. Stunning, if Megan said so herself. Glamorous, sexy even. Not the typical style she would ever considering wearing, but that had been part of the challenge. The fun. The dress wasn't doing much good hanging in her closet.

"Bring the dress in tomorrow," Eva ordered.

The thought of showing a talented costume designer like Eva Redding her dress knotted Megan's stomach. "I... I..."

"You're my intern," Eva said. "I'm not going to allow you to embarrass me and Adam by showing up at a huge media event in the wrong dress."

Good point. "I'll show you the dress tomorrow."

In his trailer, Adam played a game on one of his consoles. His cell phone beeped. A text message had arrived. He glanced at the touch screen. The text was from Megan.

Thanks for talking to Eva!!!! I can go to the awards show with you!!!!!

All the exclamation points made him smile. He typed a reply back.

Great!

Adam had looked for her this morning, but hadn't seen her. He missed her smile. He typed another text.

See you at lunch?

As soon as he pressed Send, he winced. Why was he torturing himself like this? Hanging out with a woman he couldn't have was stupid.

Her response arrived quickly.

Yes!!!!

A thrill flashed through him at the thought of being with her. What was a little bit more torture, especially when she had such gorgeous eyes and a very pretty smile and made him feel like the king of the world? Even though he knew better, he typed.

See you then!

The next day, Megan carried a garment bag containing her dress into the costume department. She was awash with nerves, but a hint of excitement that Eva might like the dress kept Megan from wigging out completely. She found most of the wardrobe crew waiting for her.

"Show us this dress of yours," Eva ordered.

With a trembling hand, Megan unzipped the bag and removed the dress. The purple fabric shimmered and sparkled. She showed the front of the dress to them.

Kenna gasped. Rosie grinned. Two others stared in disbelief.

Eva studied the gown. Her blank expression gave nothing away as to her opinion of the dress. "Show me the back."

Megan turned the dress around.

"Interesting," Eva said.

Megan had no idea if interesting was good or bad. She was afraid to ask so she kept her lips pressed together in a half smile.

"With a couple fixes, it'll work for the Viewers' Choice Awards," Eva said. "The bow has to go. The slit needs to be higher."

Megan tightened her grip on the hanger. It was already slit to her midthigh. Any higher...

"What shoes?" Eva asked.

Megan pulled out a pair of sandals. They were the dressiest shoes she owned.

Every person in the room shook their head. A few looked horrified by her choice of footwear.

"No," Eva said. "You need a higher heel. Slingbacks or a T-strap. Silver."

The others nodded their approval.

"I'll buy a pair," Megan said.

Eva shook her head. "I'll take care of it."

As Megan stood there holding her dress, her coworkers debated what accessories she needed as well as what to do with her hair and makeup. More people joined in on the discussion until a plan had been made, one without any input from her. She felt like a mannequin in a store window. Was this how Adam felt during a fitting and when he was being dressed for a shoot?

"You'll get ready here." A rare smile brightened Eva's face. "You'll be feeling like Cinderella by the time we're finished with you."

Megan wiggled her toes. She would have never believed Firebreather had it in her to be a fairy godmother. Or Adam her prince. "Thanks."

She would happily enjoy the fairy tale for the night. Even if a part of her wished it could last a little longer.

CHAPTER TEN

PRODUCTION was halfway over. Shooting continued amid delays, including an unexpected rain shower on a day scheduled for an outdoor scene. Script changes slowed. The shoot would be moving on location shortly. That would mix things up a bit and make this bubble world of the set even smaller.

Adam was looking forward to getting away from the lot. Being on location meant fewer distractions. More time to spend with Megan.

He exited the set following a close-up shot, his eyelids heavy and his feet dragging. He had an hour and a half break. He wanted to make the most of it. No video games, no phone calls, no texts. His assistant, Veronica, was making sure his bed was turned down and a white-noise machine running.

Napping wasn't his usual way to relax on the set, but a fling wasn't happening. At least not with the one woman he wanted. No one else interested him as much. At least he had a new friend.

"Adam." One of the grips ran up to him. "Chas is looking for you."

Damn. Adam didn't want to waste his break talking to the producer. Now if it were Megan... He would see her at lunch. Mealtimes were their main time together. It reminded Adam a little of high school, except students got some action. He wasn't getting any—no kisses or hand-holding even. But celibacy was turning out to be good for his acting. He could almost taste a nomination. "Tell Chas I'm getting a cup of coffee."

Adam trudged his way to the food and drinks table. He yawned, fighting a bone-weary tiredness that had set in over the past week and a half. A busy schedule and sleepless nights didn't go well together.

He downed half a cup of coffee. Maybe that would wake him up. Though it might wreak havoc with his nap.

"Looks like you could use a jolt of caffeine." Chas joined him at the coffee station. "Or a nap."

"Between the shoot and PR for the SEALs film, I don't have time to breathe." Adam had been running from one thing to the next, wherever he was told to go. The one constant amid all the chaos was Megan. She was always on his mind, day or night, awake or asleep. A little weird considering he'd kissed her only once. An air of mystery hovered around her. Maybe it was because they hadn't slept together. But with only a few weeks left of the shoot he wasn't going to analyze it too much. "I've lost track of the number of radio phone-in interviews I've done."

"Keep up whatever you're doing. The dailies look great," Chas said. "Everyone thinks I'm a genius for wanting you to play Maxwell."

Adam drank more coffee. The strong, hot drink tasted good going down his throat. "I never did ask why you were so set on me for the part."

"My wife," Chas admitted. "She's been a big fan ever since Neptune."

That one role had changed everything for him. He hoped bigger things happened with this film. "So she's the true genius."

Chas nodded. "And she knows it, too."

The sound of wheels rolling on the asphalt made Adam glance to his left. Megan pushed a clothing rack to the costume department. A camera bag hung off her shoulder. Worn jeans hugged her thighs like a second skin. A scooped-neck burgundy shirt with a sleeveless sweater over it complimented her ivory skin. More stylish than a plain T-shirt. If only she'd wear her hair down instead of clipped on the top of her head...

Megan's gaze met his.

Her beaming smile took his breath away. He waved, then watched the gentle sway of her hips as she passed by.

Chas tsked. "Texas, huh? I had no idea."

Adam's gaze jerked from Megan's retreating backside to the producer. "What was that about Texas?"

"I didn't realize the two of you were an item."

Unease slithered down his spine. "We're not."

"Could have fooled me the way her eyes lit up when she saw you."

Yeah, they had lit up. He'd noticed that a couple of times. Her smile seemed wider and brighter. It didn't mean anything. She must be getting excited about the Viewers' Choice Awards on Saturday night. Adam was looking forward to it. He'd been nominated, but he wanted to see Megan all dressed up and walking down the red carpet. "We're friends."

They were friends. Except when was the last time Adam had wanted to see a friend so much or thought about a friend all the time or dreamed about them? Hot dreams. Naked dreams. He gulped.

Chas winked. "I know what kind of friend you are, one who funds shopping sprees after a night of hot monkey sex. No wonder you're so tired lately."

The producer's wink-wink, nudge-nudge tone bothered Adam. He didn't like the insinuation that Megan might be trading sex for clothes. "We're friends, period. No sex or shopping sprees."

Chas shrugged. "Well, given the way she looks at you, if you want her, she won't put up much of an argument."

A weight pressed down on the center of Adam's chest. "Megan might surprise you."

She had surprised him. He knew the kind of romantic relationship Megan wanted. It was one hundred and eighty degrees different from what he wanted.

Maybe there was some middle ground where they both could be satisfied with more than their friendship right now. Or maybe things would continue as they were until production shut down and that would be it. They would say goodbye and move on to their next projects without looking back on what might have been. The thought of not talking to or seeing her again bummed him out. He drank the rest of his coffee.

"Hugh wants to see you," Chas said.

An image of Rhys Rogers dressed as a clown, complete with red nose and frizzy orange wig, performing at a kid's birthday party appeared in Adam's mind. Dread coupled with a sense of foreboding knotted his gut. "Hugh's never wanted to see me before."

Chas nodded. "Don't worry."

"Easy for you to say. You aren't the one rolling around in bed with Hugh's fiancée."

During yesterday's love scene shoot, Lane had her hands all over Adam. If she'd become Calliope and gotten wrapped up in the moment, he wouldn't have minded so much. But what she did had nothing to do with acting like a husband and wife making love and everything to do with Lane being a sexual predator and him her prey. Damon had been pleased with the shot, but no one, not even the watchful director, knew what Lane had been trying to do to Adam under the sheets.

Talk about awkward. He was relieved that Megan hadn't been allowed on the closed set. Nonessential crew members were kept out during sex scene shoots. A good thing because Adam hadn't wanted Megan to feel uncomfortable about his acting with Lane.

"I'm serious. No worries," Chas said. "Hugh has a favor to ask. That's all."

The studio head was rich and powerful. Adam had nothing Hugh would want or need. "When and where does he want to see me?"

"Now. In his office."

So much for a nap. Adam tossed his cup into the trash can.

"Leave it to Hugh to know this is my biggest chunk of free time until lunch."

"He knows everything that happens around here."

Adam wondered if Hugh knew what his fiancée was up to, even when the cameras were rolling. Somehow Adam doubted it.

"Hugh always reciprocates favors," Chas said in a low voice. "He's a good person to have in your debt."

"I'll keep that in mind."

Five minutes later, Adam entered Hugh Wilstead's office. Floor-to-ceiling windows along the back wall overlooked the entire lot. Movie posters covered the other walls along with a USC pennant and a Stanford flag. Framed photographs and awards filled bookshelves. Impressive.

"Hello, Adam." Hugh rose from behind a giant mahogany desk with a telephone and a laptop on top. The studio head wore a gray suit, yellow tie and white button-down shirt. Except for the patch of gray hair at his temple, he looked to be in his mid-thirties. He shook Adam's hand firmly. "Thanks for stopping by. The shoot is going well."

Adam nodded. "Solid script. Talented cast. Great crew. You're going to have a winner on your hands."

"I like your confidence." Hugh motioned to a black leather chair. "Sit."

Adam did.

Hugh sat and leaned back in his chair. "I find myself in a bit of a dilemma. I have to be in Europe this weekend. A meeting I can't get out of."

Adam had no idea what this had to do with him, but Hugh didn't sound pleased. "That's too bad."

"Lane is not happy about it," Hugh said. "When she's not happy, everyone around her will be unhappy."

So that explained Lane's tantrum this morning. At least it hadn't been because Adam had turned her down. Again. "We don't want Lane unhappy."

"That's why I need a favor."

Adam should have known this "favor" might have something to do with Lane. He doubted Hugh would want him to sleep with his fiancée. The guy didn't look like the type who shared his toys. But Hugh Wilstead was someone you wanted in your corner. Especially if they owed you a favor, as Chas had mentioned. "I'm happy to help out, what do you need?"

"The Viewers' Choice Awards are Saturday night. Lane's nominated," Hugh said. "I'd like you to escort her to the event, as a personal favor to me."

No freaking way. Adam's stomach roiled at the thought of spending the evening with Lane instead of Megan. "I have a date."

Hugh straightened. "That does complicate matters."

Adam nodded. He remembered the excitement dancing in Megan's pretty brown eyes when he'd invited her. He couldn't wait to show her the glamorous side of the movie industry. "She's excited to go. I would hate to let her down."

"No doubt," Hugh agreed. "But this is just one awards show. There will be others."

Not for months. Who knew where either of them would be by then? He couldn't imagine them together, but the thought of not being with Megan made Adam shift in his seat. He liked having her around.

Hugh's gaze hardened. "You're a smart man. You'll think of a way to make it up to her. The way I'll make it up to you."

The carrot dangled. The consequences of saying no to Hugh weighed on Adam's mind as much as the benefit of saying yes. He'd worked hard to get where he was. He didn't want to derail the momentum of his career over something like this.

But he couldn't stop thinking about Megan. She would be disappointed and rightly so. He took a deep breath, feeling trapped. No matter what he decided someone wouldn't be happy. Someone would be hurt. He didn't want that person to be Megan.

A few weeks ago, he would have said yes to Hugh without any hesitation. But the thought of hurting her tightened a vice grip around Adam's heart. She'd come to mean a lot to him. The depth of his feelings for her took him by surprise.

"This is a difficult spot to be in," Hugh continued. "We never want to let down the women we love."

Whoa. Adam clutched the chair arms. Hugh might love Lane, but Adam didn't love Megan. Okay, he liked her. Megan was nice. Pretty. Hot. He enjoyed kissing her and being with her. He cared what happened to her. But nothing would ever come of it. She wouldn't be around for long. No one ever was.

Friendship was one thing. But love…

No way. He didn't love anybody. Except his mom. And that hadn't always turned out so well with men flitting in and out of their lives. Love was uncertain, out of control and left you hurting when it went south. Which it always did.

Why would anyone want to fall in love?

He didn't plan on it, but Megan…

I want my first time to be with someone I love and trust and who feels the same way about me.

She wanted to be in love, but that didn't mean she'd fallen for him?

Could have fooled me the way her eyes lit up when she saw you.

Well, if you want her, it doesn't look like she'll put up much of an argument.

Chas noticing those things about Megan bothered Adam. He didn't want a relationship or a girlfriend. He didn't want any sort of attachments to slow down his career or put his heart at risk.

Or hers.

Megan had her whole life ahead of her and big plans, ones that would take her away from him. If she'd developed romantic feelings for him, then his not taking her to the awards ceremony would be a good thing for both their sakes. Neither of them could afford to get in too deep.

"You and Lane attending the awards will drum up early publicity for the movie," Hugh added. "It will help your SEALs film, too."

Adam found himself nodding, ignoring the voice inside his head reminding him about Megan. He'd promised her a good time. He hated breaking his promises. He remembered how badly it stung when his mother broke hers.

Hugh steepled his hands. "So I can count on you for Saturday."

It wasn't a question. Adam thought about Megan. Her expressive eyes told him what she was feeling. Her smile warmed his heart. The sound of her laughter brightened his day. The intoxicating scent of her made him dizzy with desire. With all those things in mind, Adam knew exactly what he needed to do about the awards ceremony.

"Yes, you can count on me," he said. "I'll take Lane to the Viewers' Choice Awards."

That would slow down whatever this thing was he had for Megan and keep it from going any further than friendship. He didn't like the way he kept reacting to whatever she said or did. Or the way she could always sense how he was feeling. He didn't like the way he felt off-balance when he was with her and unsettled when he wasn't.

This was for the best. Even if Adam wasn't looking forward to having to tell Megan.

In Lane Gregory's dressing room, Megan secured a diamond-encrusted watch on the actress's slim wrist. She double-checked to make sure it was fastened correctly. Dressing actresses sure beat being stuck fixing broken zippers or doing laundry after everyone went home. "Is that too tight?"

Lane moved her wrist back and forth. Her lips were set in a frown, and she'd been snapping since they arrived. "No."

While Kenna kneeled on the ground fixing the hem of Lane's skirt, Megan checked the photograph showing what the actress had worn when the previous scene had been shot.

Hair, earrings, scarf, blouse, jacket, watch, wedding ring, skirt, belt, shoes.

Scenes weren't shot in chronological order. Lane had worn this costume last week. Everything had to be the same as then.

Megan checked the photograph again. "The scarf knot is on the wrong side."

Kenna stood. "I'll fix it. Get me some double-stick tape."

Megan rummaged through their supplies of safety pins, needles, glue and anything else that might come in handy to find. A cell phone buzzed.

"Someone get that for me," Lane said.

Megan grabbed the phone off a table, then handed it to her.

As the actress read the text, her features relaxed. The frown disappeared. "Thank heavens, he came through for me."

Megan glanced at Kenna, who shrugged.

Lane handed the phone back to Megan. "Thanks, sweetie."

Definitely in a better mood after that text message. Megan placed the phone back on the table. "Good news?"

"Yes." Lane checked her reflection in the mirror. "I've been so upset since I found out my fiancé couldn't take me to the Viewers' Choice Awards."

Hearing the words *Viewers' Choice Awards* sent a thrill shooting through Megan. She couldn't wait to go. Not only to see what an awards show was like, but to spend quality time with Adam. She saw him only if their breaks and mealtimes coincided. His days off were full of personal appearances for his upcoming movie release. They might be just friends, but she missed him when they were apart.

Adam starred in her dreams. He'd pushed Rob out of her mind and made her wonder if her heart had truly ever belonged to her best friend. Or if her dreams about Rob had been one big schoolgirl fantasy she'd clung to into adulthood.

Not that she was ready to give her heart to Adam. But the thought of kissing him again had been on her mind.

"You're nominated for an award," Kenna said.

"Best actress." Lane shimmied her shoulders, sending the

scarf every which way. A good thing they had tape to secure it in place. "But my dearest, devoted Hugh came through for me."

Megan handed Kenna the tape. "He isn't going away?"

"He's still going, but he's found the perfect man to escort me to the awards ceremony." A canary-eating grin settled on Lane's face. "Adam."

Megan's heart slammed against her chest. She clutched the back of a chair to keep her knees from buckling. Not her Adam. She wanted to tell Lane she was wrong. Lane had to be wrong. "Adam?"

Lane laughed. "Adam Noble. You know, my costar and leading man."

I'm a leading man, not a best friend. You'd be wise to remember that.

His words echoed through Megan's head. But that didn't mean... It couldn't...

Adam had invited her. He'd asked Eva's permission. The entire costume department knew. There had to be some sort of mistake. "I—"

Kenna touched Megan's shoulder and sent her a compassionate yet pointed look.

"I'm sure you'll have a great time," Kenna said.

"With Adam as my date, I know I will." Lane looked at Megan. "Did you have something to say, Texas?"

"I, um, hope you win."

Lane pushed her blond hair behind her shoulders. "Me, too."

Hurt swirled through Megan, making her throat burn and her eyes sting. Adam had promised her a good time. He'd promised.

He probably figured since they were just friends, she would understand why he couldn't take her. That he had to put his career first over a friend, a woman he wasn't sleeping with. A woman who was nothing compared to a glamorous actress like Lane Gregory.

Anger burned. Megan couldn't believe Adam hadn't called her first and at least asked if she minded or cared. But he hadn't. Of course not. He was the star. Adam Noble could do whatever he wanted. And had.

Worse, this hurt more than anything with Rob ever had. Pathetic. She should have stuck to crushing on him. It might not have gone anywhere, Rob might not have made her heart go pitter-pat like Adam, but at least she wouldn't have felt like someone had done jumping jacks on her chest.

Megan wondered what excuse Adam would give her for taking Lane to the awards. She couldn't wait to find out, but one thing was certain. She doubted whatever he told her would be the truth.

A knock sounded at Adam's trailer door. He grimaced. The last thing he wanted was any company. He needed to figure out what to say to Megan. If only Veronica hadn't stepped out…

Another knock.

Adam opened the door. "Megan?"

Her mouth was set in a firm line. "May I come in?"

He motioned her inside. "What's going on?"

She took a breath, then exhaled slowly. "Lane told me you're taking her to the Viewers' Choice Awards."

Damn. He hadn't expected that to happen. "I was going to tell you."

"Then it's true?"

The disappointment in her voice hit Adam harder than a left hook to his jaw. He felt like a jerk, a selfish jerk who had made a decision solely on what he wanted and felt.

But it was for the best. He would only end up hurting Megan more in the long run. Better now while her heart wasn't tied too tightly to him. Or his…

No, that wouldn't happen. His heart was safe. He made sure it was always safe.

He moistened his dry lips. "Yes, it's true."

The color drained from her face. "I…"

Adam hated seeing her like this. The last time she'd stood in his trailer they'd kissed. He wished they could go back to that time. "I'm sorry you had to find out this way. I was going to tell you at lunch."

Flames flickered in her eyes. "That's supposed to make me feel better?"

He met her gaze. He knew she'd be upset. Now he had to own up to it. "No."

"I don't understand."

"It's not you…" As soon as he said the words he knew he shouldn't have said them. Not only because they were cliché, but also because they were a lie. His going with Lane had as much to do with Megan as it did Hugh Wilstead. Adam's mouth tasted like sand. "Lane's fiancé is a powerful man."

"I might be only an intern, but I know all about Hugh Wilstead."

"Then you know when he asks you to do something, you do it or pay the consequences," Adam explained. "I've worked too hard to get where I am to screw up everything now by refusing."

She raised her chin. "So you did this for your career?"

Not completely. A Golden Globe–size lump of guilt lodged in his throat. No way could he tell her the entire reason, of how her feelings and his had played into his decision-making. He'd been more open with Megan than any other woman—person—in his life. But he wasn't going to share that. He…couldn't.

"This is how Hollywood works," he explained instead. "Costars go to awards shows and premieres together. Some go as far as pretending to date. It's part of show business."

She didn't say anything, but blinked. Her eyes glistened.

Damn, he didn't want her to cry. "I know how much you wanted to go to the awards. You can still go. I'll get you a ticket."

She shook her head. "I want to go to the awards, but I wanted to go with you."

Her disillusionment in him was clear. He'd let her down. Big-time. But it couldn't be helped.

"I'm sorry," he said. "I'll make it up to you. I promise."

A shopping spree on Rodeo Drive would be good. She liked clothes. He would love to see her try on some sexy cocktail dresses and a bikini or two.

Love?

No, he wouldn't like that. Veronica could take her shopping instead.

Megan arched a brow. "Like you promised me I'd have a good time at the awards ceremony? No thanks."

His gut clenched. "Megan…"

"Eva was right about actors playing by different rules."

"I said I was sorry, what else do you want from me?"

"Nothing," she said firmly. "I get being friends with the costume intern is awkward. But I thought that was okay because you seemed more grounded than some of the other talent on the set. But I realize you live in one world. I live in another. Maybe we would have been better off keeping it that way."

"That might have been the smart thing to do, but we didn't."

"We still could."

"No." The word rushed from his mouth before he knew what he was saying.

"Why not?" She eyed him curiously. "It's not like we're BFFs."

They weren't, but Adam didn't want to say goodbye to her. "We're still friends."

"Are we?" Confusion filled her voice. Her lower lip trembled. "The truth is, I've been wondering whether we could be more than friends. But now I realize how foolish that line of thinking was."

Damn. Letting her go was the best thing Adam could do for both of them, but that didn't stop him from reaching for her. "Megan."

She backed away. "There's nothing left for us to say."

With that, she exited his trailer.

He plopped into a chair, feeling more alone than he'd ever felt in his life.

CHAPTER ELEVEN

Two days later, Megan stood in the workroom sorting through the dry cleaning she'd picked up earlier. Wardrobe pieces needed to be labeled and organized. Tedious work, but detail oriented. It kept her distracted, something she needed right now.

She yawned, stretching her arms over her head. She needed more coffee or an energy drink to get her through the day after not sleeping well last night.

Megan ripped off the plastic covering a crisp, white button-down oxford shirt that had been laundered and lightly starched. She removed the cleaner's inventory number stapled to the tag, relabeled the shirt with the character name, Maxwell, and scene number seventeen so she could stick the clothes in the proper garment bag and hung it on the rack. Adam's rack. She grimaced.

She didn't want to think about him, but traces of him were everywhere. Here and at home.

A bouquet of wildflowers had been sitting by her front door when she arrived home the day she found out about his taking Lane instead. A note card had been attached.

"Let me make this up to you."

Nothing more than Adam feeling obligated to make amends like he had with lunch after they'd met. Well, that was his problem, not hers. She had given the flowers to her neighbor, Mrs. Hamilton. The tears glistening in the elderly woman's blue eyes let Megan know she'd made the right choice giving the flowers away.

But she had been serious about not wanting anything from Adam. She wanted to put this behind her, move on and…grow up.

Being disappointed was one thing. But that had been part of her daily life for as long as she'd been alive. When her older sister, Jess, the Golden Girl of Larkville, had gotten herself knocked up by a man who wanted nothing to do with her or their baby, Megan had thought her mother would see her differently, perhaps more positively. Instead, her mother had said she always thought Megan would be the one coming home pregnant, not Jess. Even when Megan did everything right, she was still wrong.

What bothered her most about what happened with Adam was how she'd ended up feeling so hurt over this. Going to the Viewers' Choice Awards would have been fun and an interesting experience. But the excitement she felt, the anticipation of Saturday night, revolved around Adam, not the awards show.

Yes, Adam had been a jerk the way he handled this. He couldn't help that she'd heard from Lane, but he still hadn't been planning to tell Megan about it until lunchtime, a few hours late. That was inconsiderate. But knowing her father, her brothers and Rob, she got that men didn't always think like women. Their sense of timing seemed off. Case in point, Rob.

She also understood that Adam had a choice to make. He chose his career. Yes, it sucked to be her in this instance. She didn't like what he'd done. But if push came to shove wouldn't she have made the same choice? She'd told Eva as much.

What was she to Adam, anyway? Not his girlfriend. Not his best friend. Not a close friend if you went by how long they'd known each other and the amount of time they'd spent together. She would have been his date for one night. Nothing more.

The bitter truth stung because Megan had wanted to believe it could be more. Different. Better. But it was just like…

Rob.

Realization washed over her with hurricane force winds. Her legs wobbled. She leaned back against a table.

What a fool she'd been.

Megan had taken all her wishful thinking about Rob and transferred it onto Adam. Another crush on a friend. Dreaming about what could be rather than the reality of the situation. Pretending things would change when they never would.

She was still the same little girl who loved to escape into animated princess movies where the evil mother—make that stepmother—would be defeated, the princess would be rescued by a handsome prince and all would live happily ever after.

None of what she'd been feeling and thinking had been any more real than the fairy-tale cartoons. Not with Rob. Definitely not with Adam.

In some ways, Megan was still trying to do what her mother wanted. Fit in and gain respectability so she wouldn't be seen as odd or different. With Rob, the grandson of the mayor. And with Adam, the handsome movie star and lead actor on the set.

She straightened and squared her shoulders.

No more.

No more crushes.

No more wanting what she couldn't make happen.

She didn't need anyone to define her or give her respectability or help her fit in. She could do all those things herself. She should have a long time ago.

But it was never too late to start.

She tore the plastic wrap off a purple silk blouse. One of Lane's wardrobe pieces.

Megan swallowed a sigh. Moving forward, she reminded herself.

Kenna and Rosie burst into the workroom with laughter and glowing faces. The two looked like they had won the lottery.

Rosie waved a white envelope in the air. "You're not going to believe this!"

Megan hung the purple shirt on a rack so it wouldn't wrinkle. "What is it?"

Kenna rubbed her hands together. "Three tickets to the Viewers' Choice Awards. One for each of us. They're up in the balcony, but who cares? We get to go!"

Rosie bounced from foot to foot. "Plus we're on the lists for the after-parties and have a limo at our disposal for the entire night. We'll be living the high life."

The sinking feeling in her stomach told Megan where this high life had probably come from. "Adam."

Rosie touched Megan's arm. "Please don't let what happened with Adam stop you from going out. Our having a blast doesn't have anything to do with him."

Megan stared at the tickets. "I told Adam I wanted nothing from him."

"So? He's given all three of us something." Kenna grinned. "He's obviously trying to get back on your good side."

Megan wasn't going there. "More likely trying to assuage a guilty conscience."

"Who cares what his reasons are?" Rosie did a little dance. "We're going to the awards show. We have our own seats. We can get into the after-parties. Nothing else matters."

Uncertainty rushed through Megan like water released from one of the dams on the Rio Grande. "I don't know."

"Well, I do," Kenna said firmly. "You're disappointed. I would be, too. But you've put on a brave face and haven't been all mopey or let it interfere with your work."

Megan knew throwing herself a pity party wouldn't solve anything so she'd thrown herself into work.

"That's how it's done in Texas." She had no idea what was happening back home on the ranch. Or Austin. She hadn't heard from Rob since he let her know he'd received Adam's autographed picture. Truth was, she didn't miss hearing from him. Her feelings for Rob weren't as deep as she originally thought. Rob was safe, stable and familiar, not the love of her life.

As much as she longed to escape Larkville, she now realized she'd wanted something to keep her connected. Otherwise, she feared she would be all on her own. Her parents were dead. Her siblings were too busy with their own lives. That was where Rob had come in. He'd shown interest. Made her feel wanted. So had Adam. But she wasn't wanted. Not by her family or Rob or…Adam.

"My dad used to say everything happens for a reason. This is no different." Maybe what happened with Adam was so she'd figure out what had been going on all these years with Rob. And with her. "I think the two of you should go and have a great time. Tony can use my ticket. I'm going to sit this one out."

"You are not sitting this one out," Eva announced from the doorway of the workroom.

When had she showed up? Megan hadn't noticed her standing there.

Eva strode into the room as if she owned the place. Given she was the costumer designer on the shoot she sort of did. "You're going to the awards show, but not with Kenna or Rosie."

Megan stared in confusion. "Adam—"

"You're not going with him, either," Eva interrupted. "My godson, Zachary Carleton, will be your escort. He's been nominated for Best Action Hero and his date had to have her appendix removed. Her loss is your gain."

Kenna shook her head. "Nothing like this ever happened to me when I was interning."

Rosie nodded.

Zach Carleton was an up-and-coming handsome actor who was around Megan's age. Hot didn't begin to describe him. She wanted to pinch herself to see if she were dreaming. "I appreciate all that you've done for me, Eva, but I have to be honest. I don't understand why."

Eva's eyes softened. "Once upon a time, a young costume designer fell in love with an older handsome actor. She thought he'd fallen for her, too, but instead he got bored and the costume designer was fired."

Megan's mouth gaped. "You?"

Eva nodded once. "But I didn't handle myself as professionally as you have. These past few days you've shown what you're made of. And after seeing your gown, it's obvious you have talent. You deserve to go to the awards and sit up front."

A chill shivered down Megan's spine. "I don't want to embarrass your godson. I'm going to be so nervous."

"It's okay to be nervous," Eva counseled. "Just don't let it show. Whatever you do, don't drink too much during the day and especially before the show starts. You don't want to have to spend all your time in the ladies' room and miss the fun. Because I can guarantee you're going to have the most wonderful time. Zachary will see to it."

Firebreather *was* a fairy godmother. "Thanks, Eva."

"Be here at eleven o'clock on Saturday morning," Eva said. "By the time we're finished with you, Mr. Adam Noble is going to be kicking himself for taking the wrong princess to the ball."

Outside the Shrine Auditorium, Adam held Lane's hand as she exited the limousine. Her fingers were thin and bony. He wished he were holding Megan's hand.

Don't go there. Stay in the moment. The cameras are rolling.

The sound of applause and camera shutters going off filled the afternoon air. Things started early on the west coast so the show could be shown in prime time on the east coast.

A female shrieked.

A chorus of women yelled, "Neptune!"

Lane raised a brow. "Such devoted fans."

With a smile in place, he waved at the ladies. "The best fans in the world."

The hem of Lane's gold-colored gown swished around her feet. Her gold, jewel-encrusted designer shoes—she'd told him in the limousine how much Hugh had paid for them—added four inches to her height, but she was still half a foot shorter than Adam. Diamonds dripped from her ears, wrist and neck. More presents from Hugh, Adam assumed, but Lane hadn't said. The magic of double-stick tape kept the extremely low-cut bodice from allowing a wardrobe malfunction, much to the dismay of males in attendance. All except Adam. He wasn't interested. Now if it were Megan…

He forced his attention back to the red carpet.

When he released her hand, Lane didn't let go. "Smile at the cameras, darling."

He pasted on his most charming smile, one he'd practiced and perfected over the past two years. A photo-shoot smile that had graced many a magazine cover. If Megan had been his date, his smile would have been real.

Don't think about it. Her.

Two steps down the red carpet reporters tossed questions at them like Frisbees on the beach.

"Where's Hugh?"

"Who designed your dress?"

"Is it true your onscreen romance has become an offscreen one?"

"Are you wearing an Armani tux?"

"How's the shoot going?"

"Are you excited about the premiere of *Navy SEALs?*"

Adam's smile didn't falter as he answered questions. His fans watched the red carpet shows on television so he didn't rush through the gauntlet, but strolled at a snail's pace from reporter to reporter.

Lane rose up on her tiptoes to whisper in his ear. "Isn't this fun?"

Every minute with Lane sucked five minutes of life out of him. But this was part of the job. Movie magic carried over to life in Hollywood. Much of it wasn't real. Pretend couples, public relation lies, phony smiles, sucking up. Whatever he said would be repeated back to Hugh Wilstead so Adam had to be careful and keep his guard up. That took all the fun out right there. "Superfun."

"Make the most of it." A twinge of desperation sounded in Lane's voice. "If they don't all want you, you're done."

No wonder she went after her male costars. She needed to be the queen of the set to prove she was still desirable. That she wouldn't be tossed aside by someone newer and prettier. That was why she'd had Annie fired. Jealousy.

Adam never would have thought he'd feel sorry for Lane, but he did.

Behind them at the beginning of the red carpet, a flurry of activity announced a new arrival. The high-pitched female screams were deafening.

"One of those teen idols must have arrived. The girls always go crazy for them." Lane waved to a girl in the crowd, who stared at the actress with total adoration. "Is it anyone we should bother saying hello to?"

Adam glanced back to see Zach Carleton signing autographs. Security was holding back crying girls. There'd been ongoing discussions about Zach and Adam playing brothers in an action movie that had been green-lighted, but the two had never met. "It's that new kid. Zach C. He's up for Best Action Actor."

Adam knew this because he'd never been nominated for an individual acting award before. Best Kiss—he'd won twice. Best Ensemble—Neptune. Best Onscreen Couple—he'd know if he won that later tonight.

"Oh, he's cute. Young, but lots of staying power." Lane smirked as she waved to more fans. "Or so I've been told. Who's he with?"

Adam glanced back. Zach held on to the hand of a woman with long, dark curly hair as she pirouetted, showing off a sexy shimmering purple gown with an even sexier slit up the side. The woman was jaw-droppingly gorgeous and young like the actor.

Adam took a closer look. She almost looked like… His heart stalled. It was. Megan. He exhaled a sharp breath.

"What?" Lane asked.

Zach rested his hand at the small of Megan's back.

Adam's jaw tightened.

Zach whispered something into her ear. She smiled shyly.
Zach laughed.

A wave of jealousy crashed through Adam like a sneaker
wave.

The two looked cozy, comfortable with each other like a...
couple.

Adam's blood pressure spiked.

"Oh, my..." Lane sounded like she had seen a badly de-
composed body. "Look at the way his ascot matches her dress.
Purple shimmers, really? It's all so senior prom-ish."

Maybe, but in a refreshing, wholesome, appealing way.
Megan captivated him. It looked like Zach felt the same way.

Adam could hardly swallow. Sweat dripped down his back.
"They're young. Attractive. It works. The press seems to agree
given the attention they're getting."

"Well, I'm not impressed." Lane blew a kiss to the fans in
the grandstand. "Zach's date looks familiar. She must be one
of those television actresses."

Adam waved to the crowd, but his gaze kept straying to
Megan. He couldn't help himself. "She's not an actress."

Lane struck a pose for a photographer. "I recognize her
from somewhere."

"She's Eva's intern." The words barely made it past the
lump in his throat.

Lane froze. "Texas?"

Adam nodded, afraid if he said anything he'd reveal how
upset he felt.

She glanced back at the couple that had barely moved two
feet due to all the attention they were receiving. "How did she
end up with him? Looking like *that*? Here?"

Adam knew Megan had been hiding something, but he
hadn't realized it was this. "I have no idea."

But he intended to find out.

Megan felt like Cinderella at the ball. She'd been feted on the
red carpet, allowed to talk about the gown she'd designed for

herself with a fashion reporter, made to feel like a fairy princess by her charming escort, Zach. He even kissed her on the cheek when he won the award for Best Action Actor.

Now she was at an after-party with Zach thrown by a top studio. No expense had been spared with the elaborate decorations. An award-winning DJ mixed the music. Stars from television, music and film filled the dance floor. Rosie, Kenna and Tony were here, but Megan had lost track of them for the umpteenth time that night.

She held on to Zach's hand, mindful of the other dancers around them. "Tonight has been magical. I feel like Cinderella."

He grinned. "Except there's no reason to be home by midnight. I can assure you the limo won't turn into a pumpkin."

As he twirled her around, one of her shoes flew off. She would find it after the song ended.

"I owe my godmother for finding me such a beautiful date," Zach said.

She stared up at him. "Thank you."

She did like Zach, but unfortunately she just didn't feel any sparks. Only friendship.

"I wish I didn't have to fly back to the shoot and be there for the next three months," he said. "It would probably sound stupid to ask you to wait for me."

Affection for Zach grew. The kind she had for her brothers. "Not stupid. Extremely sweet."

Hope filled his eyes.

"Who knows where I'll be or what I'll be doing in three months. Same with you. But you've got my cell number," she said honestly. "Give me a ring when you're back in town."

By then he'd surely have found someone else to pin his hopes on.

He nodded enthusiastically. "I will."

The music came to an end. A man waved at Zach. "Would you mind if I said hello to someone?"

He really was a nice guy. Younger than her, but very cute. "Go ahead."

As Zach pushed his way through the crowd to reach his friend, Megan searched for her missing shoe, hobbling with one shoe on, being careful so she wouldn't twist an ankle. She searched the dance floor, but didn't see it.

Where could her shoe be?

Adam appeared at her side.

Her heart danced a jig. He looked so handsome in his tux. Tom Ford, if she wasn't mistaken.

"Lose your date?" he asked.

"He's saying hello to a friend. But I did lose a shoe."

Adam pulled something from behind his back. He held up her silver slingback heel, the match to the one on her foot. Eva and the wardrobe department had purchased the shoes for Megan. A gift for their favorite intern, they'd claimed. She reminded them she was their only intern.

Megan reached for the shoe. "Thank you so much."

He pulled it out of her reach. "I've got it."

As Adam kneeled, she stuck out her leg, toes pointed. Her purple nail polish glimmered in the light from the ballroom chandeliers. He gently placed the shoe on her foot. As he pulled on the strap, his thumb brushed her ankle, sending a rush of sensation up her leg.

Her temperature surged.

"How's that?" he asked.

She cleared her dry throat. "Fine."

Adam stood. He held out his hand, palm up. "Dance with me."

Temptation flared. She shouldn't. "Our dates—"

"Are off with others," he interrupted. "What's one dance between friends? I do consider myself your friend even if you don't think so."

Megan wasn't ready to have this conversation. If she danced with him, she wouldn't have to talk to him. "One dance."

She placed her hand on top of his. Adam led her onto the dance floor.

"You're the most beautiful woman here tonight." He took

her into his arms. His hand rested possessively at the small of her back, pressing her close while he held her other hand. His thumb stroked her palm, sending little pleasurable thrills sliding over her.

"Thank you," she said, awash in sensation. She hated the way her body reacted to him. "I had lots of help."

His gaze raked over her. "The dress?"

"I made it, but others refined my design."

Appreciation warmed his green eyes. "Stunning."

"I'm happy how it came out."

"I'm jealous."

She drew back. "Excuse me?"

"No favor is worth seeing you with another man." Contrition echoed in his voice. "I should have never agreed to bring Lane."

A mix of emotion swirled through Megan. She wished his words didn't bring her so much pleasure. She needed to be cautious around him. But she also knew she would remember this moment, this dance, forever. "Some lessons are hard to learn."

Desire shone in his gaze. "I won't make the same mistake twice. Come on."

Holding on to her hand, he led her off the dance floor and into an alcove outside the grand ballroom. Megan didn't want to cause a scene so went with him.

As soon as she knew they couldn't be seen, she pulled her hand out of his. "What do you think you're doing?"

"It's time I admit defeat," he said. "I want you."

She half laughed, half choked, a reaction based on a combination of nerves and self-preservation. "This isn't the real me."

"I know who you are." Adam's appreciative gaze traveled the length of her. "The way you look now. That part has always been inside or you would have never made the dress. You've been too nervous, too scared, to show anybody who you really are. In Larkville, in college and here."

Adam knew who she was. He understood her. The realization pleased her as much as it scared her. Crushing on Rob had been safe. Adam was proving to be as dangerous as she'd originally thought.

"I've seen the real you," he continued. "I like what I see. And I'm finally ready to admit that."

Her heart pounded double-time to the music in the ballroom. If the rapid tattoo of her heartbeat continued too long she might hyperventilate. A part of her wanted to flee, to pretend none of this had ever happened. It was too risky, too dangerous to her peace of mind, to her heart.

But the look in Adam's eyes held her captive. She couldn't have moved if she wanted to. But she also couldn't forget the way he'd acted and treated her.

Megan stared down her nose at him. "So you're going to apologize and call it good? And when it happens again? And again—"

"I've been a lousy friend." He sounded sincere. "I'm sorry about that, but when I'm around you I don't always think straight."

That she understood. Being near him seemed to short-circuit her brain. "I know the feeling."

"I want us to try again."

All the reasons this was a bad idea shouted inside her head at once, the noise deafening. But she couldn't deny the excitement pulsing through her at the same time. "At being friends?"

He nodded. "We have to start somewhere if we're ever going to be more than friends."

Her lips parted in surprise.

More than friends.

The words echoed through her trembling heart. Dare she hope?

Adam lowered his mouth. He kissed her with a hunger that took her breath away and left her wanting more. This wasn't a practice kiss. There was no script he was following this time. The kiss was…real.

She clung to him for support and strength and more kisses. He left no doubt in her mind that he wanted her.

Megan couldn't deny she wanted him.

He wrapped his arms around her and pulled her closer. Megan went willingly. Her hands splayed his back. She relished in the moment, in the sensations pulsating through her. Kissing Adam was all that mattered. Being with him made her happy.

She pressed harder against his lips, exploring his mouth with her tongue. With each passing second, the heat intensified. An ache built deep within her. She wanted more, so much more.

A moan escaped her lips. At least she thought it came from her mouth, but she wasn't certain.

Adam dragged his lips from hers. The desire in his eyes matched her own. He seemed as shaken as her.

Her lips burned from his kiss. She fought the urge to touch them. "Why did you kiss me like that?"

"Why did you kiss me back?"

Her cheeks burned. A part of her wished she were still kissing him. "I asked my question first."

He traced her lips with his fingertips, sending goose bumps down her arms. "You mentioned you'd thought about us being more than friends. I wanted to show you what that might be like. Pretty good, huh?"

Awesome was the only word to describe it, but Megan couldn't let Adam know that. She didn't want to lose herself in another fantasy world. She needed to stick to reality and real relationships.

But Adam's kisses had felt real. Tingles were still shooting through her. Maybe her feelings for him weren't a crush as they'd been with Rob. Heaven knew, they felt more real and grounded in something true between them. "Mission accomplished."

Mischief shone in his eyes. "I was hoping it might take a little more convincing."

Megan was so tempted. "We're here with other dates."

Adam grinned. "I take full responsibility for that. But another kiss—"

"Zach and Lane might be wondering where we are." The

words spewed from Megan's mouth faster than a bucking bronc into the rodeo arena. She was truly flattered, but nervous. "They might be looking for us."

"I'm not going to let this drop."

She didn't want him to let it drop, but she needed time to think about things. About him. And what she wanted or didn't want. She had to be careful. "I know."

"I want a second chance."

"I know that, too." She moistened her swollen lips. "I'm not sure us being more than friends makes sense right now."

"Think about more kisses and other stuff we could be doing together."

Disappointment shot a hole through the haze of desire still pulsating through her. "I'm not up for a fling."

"I don't do long-term."

She sighed. "I'm not sure where that leaves us."

"We can agree to make the most of the time we have together during the shoot," he suggested. "You should learn how to have fun and date. That doesn't have to mean sex, but it can mean more kissing. I can show you what romance is all about."

Megan knew there was more to being with a movie star than red carpets and dancing. Keeping sex out of the equation would allow them to get to know each other while they were busy working on the shoot. But she couldn't forget one thing. "Eva—"

"Or not so much kissing and romance." He didn't hesitate at all. "I'm okay with that, as long as we're spending time together. But it's totally up to you."

No one had ever given Megan a decision like this to make. She liked the way it made her feel. Empowered. Reckless. "Let's make the most of the time we have left. I'm willing to have fun and see where this goes."

Adam grinned. "Sounds good to me."

Megan, too. She just hoped she wasn't making a big mistake....

CHAPTER TWELVE

By the time production moved out of Los Angeles and on location outside of Albuquerque, New Mexico, Adam couldn't have been happier with Megan giving him a second chance. Her sweet personality and sense of humor kept a big smile on his face. He wanted to keep things uncomplicated, but occasionally and only in the privacy of his trailer where they had no chance of being seen, they shared sizzling hot kisses.

Once the shoot finished, they would move on to other projects in different locales. But Adam wondered if they might keep seeing each other still. Perhaps spend a few days together back in L.A. or have Megan visit him on the set of his next film.

He walked to his trailer parked outside an old school being used as a prison. Each step brought a puff of dirt flying into the air. No wonder Megan had been up half the night doing laundry; keeping costumes clean was a full-time job.

"Adam," Lane called after him.

He groaned inwardly, but stopped and waited for her to catch up to him. "Hey."

She smiled up at him. "You killed it today."

He ignored the flirtation in her voice. The woman never gave up. "Thanks."

"I was wondering if you wanted to have dinner tonight?" Lane asked. "I heard there's a steak house about twenty minutes from here."

Funny, but he thought he'd heard her say she didn't eat red

meat. Guess she hated being stuck out in the middle of no-where so maybe she was willing to expand what she ate. But no matter what the reason for her invitation, he wasn't going anywhere with her. "Thanks, but I can't."

Adam was having dinner with Megan. He couldn't wait to see her when she returned to the set from the motel. No doubt tired from having to wash so many clothes. Maybe she'd want a back rub. He bit back a grin. He didn't want Lane thinking his smile was meant for her.

She scrunched her nose unattractively. "What's your excuse this time? You have a date?"

Adam was tired of dealing with her. He rocked back on his heels. "Yeah, I do."

Her mouth gaped. "With who?"

When he didn't answer, Lane named several costars and female crew members.

"Nope," he said.

"That only leaves…Texas." Lane made a face. "Please tell me you aren't dating that lowly intern."

Intern, yes. Lowly, no way. Megan had more class in her little finger than Lane had in her entire body. "Okay, I won't tell you."

With that, Adam walked away. Lane yelled his name, but he didn't turn around. The shoot had only a couple more weeks to go. But he'd put up with enough from Lane Gregory. Maybe this would get her off his back once and for all. He hoped so because the only woman he wanted to think and worry about was…Megan.

Megan tested the iron on a white motel pillowcase. She'd spent the morning washing clothes. Scorching a piece of wardrobe would not be good and being forced to make a mad dash to re-place something didn't appeal to her in the slightest, not when she could be spending time with Adam.

Ever since the party after the Viewers' Choice Awards things had been going well. She was getting to know him and understand him. She felt comfortable with him. She'd been thinking this could turn into something…more.

The iron seemed fine. No marks were on the pillowcase. She grabbed one of the prison jumpsuits. She'd iron out the wrinkles. Then put the ones from the last scene back in.

The joys of continuity and out of sequence shots.

Four hours later, she turned off and unplugged the iron. Mission accomplished. The prison garb was finished. She could return to the set. And Adam.

Anticipation shot through her. She'd missed him today.

As she cleaned up and put things away, she heard footsteps outside the motel. A knock sounded.

That was odd. Everyone from the shoot should be on the set. Must be the motel manager.

Megan opened the door. "Eva."

The designer's face looked pale and drawn. She wouldn't meet Megan's eyes.

"Is everything okay?" Megan asked.

Eva entered the room and closed the door behind her. "No, it's not."

Megan's first thought was something bad happened on the set. To Adam. She dug her fingernails into her palms. "What's wrong?"

"You've been fired."

Fired? Megan stared at Eva in disbelief. No one had voiced any complaints or suggested Megan wasn't doing a good job. She hadn't been late to one of her calls or taken any sick days. "Why?"

Compassion filled Eva's eyes. "One of the lead actors demanded it."

The air rushed from Megan's lungs. Her stomach knotted. Her knees threatened to give out. She plopped onto one of the double-size beds in the motel room. "Not…"

She couldn't say his name. A weight pressed down on the center of her chest, making it hard to breathe.

"Not Adam," Eva said.

Relief nearly knocked her to her knees. Megan shouldn't have doubted him for a minute. But if not him... "Lane Gregory."

Eva nodded once.

Megan's shoulders sagged. "I don't understand. I haven't worked with her much, but when I did she was always nice to me. Why would she have me fired?"

"Jealousy."

She drew back. "Lane has no reason to be jealous of me."

"You're young, talented, thin and pretty. Sometimes that's all it takes. But in this case, you've also caught Adam's eye. Lane doesn't like that because she wants him all to herself."

"She's engaged."

"Hollywood is a world unto itself. Things happen here that wouldn't happen anywhere else," Eva explained. "If it's any consolation, Adam went to bat for you. I was impressed with how he took on Hugh Wilstead. But Hugh sided with Lane."

Numbness set in. At least Adam had tried. Fought for her. That counted for something. Okay, a lot. "So what happens now?"

"You need to gather your things, pack and fly back to L.A."

"My internship?"

Eva shook her head. "I'm sorry. The work I need done is here."

Emotion clogged Megan's throat. She'd worked so hard only to have the internship end because of a jealous actress. Her throat burned, but she wasn't going to cry. She needed to be professional about this. She raised her chin. "I understand."

And she did.

Megan had been warned about getting involved with the talent. She'd been told a lead actor could have anyone fired at any time for any reason. But she hadn't realized it could turn out *this* way. That a woman engaged to another man would be jealous of Megan's relationship with Adam. She'd naively thought things would work out okay.

What was she going to do?

The thought of leaving Adam and returning to Larkville made her nauseous. She wrapped her arms around her stomach. "I was hoping my internship could lead to something more permanent. I don't want to go back to Texas."

"Then don't."

Her gaze met Eva's. The fierceness in the designer's blue eyes made Megan's heart pound.

"Don't let a jealous harpy like Lane Gregory stop you from going after what you want," Eva said. "You have the talent. You have a little experience now. You also have connections. Make the most of them."

Megan did have those things. Most important she had Adam. Not that she'd ask him to find her a job, but maybe he could introduce her to some costume designers. "Thanks, Eva. I've learned a lot."

"You've done a lot." Eva's eyes gleamed. "Leave the costumes in here. I'll have Kenna take care of them. As soon as you finish packing, a car will take you to the airport."

"Seriously?"

"Lane demands it. She claims you are too big a distraction on the set."

This was unbelievable. "Can I say goodbye to everyone?"

"You're not allowed back on the set."

Everybody was there. Including Adam. Her hands trembled. "Will you tell people goodbye for me?"

"Yes."

That was something. "What happens when I get back to L.A.?"

"Relax for a couple of days. Rewrite your résumé. Contact everyone you've met in the business and let them know you're looking for any kind of costume or wardrobe position. Feel free to use me as a reference."

"Thanks." Megan appreciated the advice, but she realized she was as much on her own here as she had been in Larkville. Forcing herself to breathe, she went to the closet and pulled out her suitcase.

Ever since arriving in Los Angeles her life had revolved around the shoot. She knew no one who wasn't working on the film except her neighbor, Mrs. Hamilton. Megan never had looked for a job. She didn't know how to begin.

But she would have to figure it out. Maybe Adam would know what she should do. Megan hoped so because she hadn't a clue. Worse, she wouldn't be able to see him for a couple of weeks. Those were going to be the longest weeks of her life.

Damn. Lane hadn't wasted any time. Adam charged through the entrance of the small airport in this middle-of-nowhere town.

He'd fought for Megan, even stood up to Hugh Wilstead during a heated conference call with Lane, Eva and Chas. Damon was too busy with the shoot to deal with something like this.

So much for being owed a favor. Hugh hadn't listened to a word Adam said. The cuckolded producer had bent over backward to appease his jealous fiancée. Adam's efforts had only meant he hadn't been able to comfort Megan and drive her to the airport. But he was here now to see her off and say…

Goodbye.

He had to say it. Do it.

Twice now, Megan had gotten hurt being with him. First the awards show and now being fired. He kept putting his own selfish desires ahead of what Megan needed. He needed to protect her. That meant letting her go.

His shoes echoed on the tile floor. The place was nearly empty except for uniformed workers and a lone, dejected-looking woman sitting in a chair with luggage at her feet.

"Megan."

She jumped out of the chair and into his open arms. "I'm so happy you're here."

He hugged her, wanting to hold her one last time. "I'm so sorry."

Megan wrapped her arms around him. "Eva told me you fought for me to stay. Thank you."

"Lane is psychotic. It'll be better if you're away from her."

Megan looked up at him with red-rimmed eyes. "But that means I'll be away from you."

Her vulnerability sliced into him like a knife's blade. He wanted to pick her up and cradle her on his lap so he could kiss her until the hurt disappeared from her face and a smile returned. But if he did that, she'd experience more hurt. He couldn't allow that to happen. "The shoot's almost finished."

Megan rose on her tiptoes and brushed her lips across his.

So tender. So sweet. Nothing would keep them apart back in L.A. Not Eva and her rule. Not Lane. They could be together finally and take things to the next level.

No, they couldn't. He couldn't.

Adam stepped back. "Megan…"

She stared up at him. "I'll be counting the days until you're back in L.A."

Adam took another step back. "I'm only going to be there for a day or two, then I'm going on location for a new project."

"Oh."

The one word spoke volumes. He hated letting her down the way other men had let down his mother. "The shoot will last three, maybe four months."

Confusion added to the hurt in her eyes. "But…"

Adam wanted to look away, but he couldn't. She was always so honest and open. He wanted to be, too. "This has been fun, but we said we'd make the most of our time together."

"And now that's over."

Over. That sounded so final. Better this way, he reminded himself. Better for Megan. "We agreed."

"I know, but I thought…"

The slight quaver in her voice knotted his gut. He wanted to know what she'd been thinking. "What?"

"Nothing," she said. "I was wrong to expect more. I see now you never intended this to be more than one of your flings."

"It wasn't a fling. We didn't have sex." But they had hung out and kissed. Really hot kisses. And grown closer, closer than he'd been to any other woman. He swallowed. "I like you a lot. I was thinking we could keep hanging out whenever I'm in L.A. We're young, there's nothing wrong with just having fun."

"But there could be so much more than that between us."

However tempting that sounded, he wouldn't allow himself to be swayed. "My life is... I'm no good for you."

Her eyes darkened. "What you really mean is continuing what we have would be too complicated."

"I'm not looking to settle down."

"The easier, the better."

"Nothing wrong with easy," he agreed.

"Except the best things in life aren't easy. They take effort and a lot of work." Her jaw tensed. "It's interesting how you work so hard to perfect your roles, but you couldn't care less about putting that same kind of effort into your relationships."

He had to be strong for both their sakes. He put his hands up, as if to hold her at bay. "We're friends. We aren't having a relationship."

She pursed her lips. "That's only because you're too afraid. You like to end things before they go bad."

He hated how her words hit the bull's-eye. "I end them when it's time."

"The shorter the relationship, I mean, fling, the better." Her sharp tone surprised him. "That's why you're backing off, because you can finally see something that could be long-term."

"I don't do long-term." He saw she expected a lot from him, more than he was willing or capable of giving. She deserved to have what she wanted. "You're better off without me."

"So who would I be better with? Zach?"

Thinking of Megan with another man ripped out Adam's guts. "No way."

"Rob?"

"He's the wrong guy for you."

"Who's the right one, then?" she pressed. "I thought it was you."

Her words stabbed his heart, but Adam couldn't let her see

how much she'd come to mean to him, as a friend and more. He'd allowed Megan to see more of him than he had with any other person. What if he pursued something with her? Then she decided to leave him rather than him being the one to leave? It wasn't a risk worth taking because people always left. No one had ever stuck around him and his mom. Not his dad. Not any of the other men who claimed they wanted to be his father, but really didn't.

"Look at me," Adam said for his benefit as much as hers. "My life is crazy. Being followed by the paparazzi, traveling all over the world for months at a time, doing whatever extreme sports I can. You have an amazing talent. You don't want to tangle up your life with someone like me. Face it. I'm not a picket-fence kind of guy. You'd only end up unhappy with me."

"Wow, all this so I'll be happier."

"I want what's best for you."

She narrowed her gaze. "What if I don't want a picket-fence life? What if I want a costume design career that takes me on location for months at a time while shooting a film and gives me the opportunity to do exciting things, also?"

He couldn't afford to believe what she said. "If that kind of life is what you really want, then you need someone more solid to be your anchor when it's time for you to come home."

"Is that what you need?"

He needed her. If only… "I'm doing fine on my own."

"You'd do better with me." Her gaze didn't waver from his. "I want you to be my anchor. I can be yours."

"I've hurt you twice," Adam said. "You even lost your internship because of me. It's best if you move on from all the trouble I've brought you."

"Have you forgotten you're the one who said he wanted a second chance with me?"

"I haven't forgotten. I had my second chance, now it's time to move on." He tried to sound flippant. He wasn't sure if he succeeded. "You need to learn that not every fun time with a guy leads to more than friendship."

"Unbelievable." She laughed. "So far, you've been the best friend, the bad boy and now the protector. Which character are you going to play next?"

His muscles tightened. "What are you talking about?"

"You're searching for excuses," she said. "You act all brave when it comes to your extreme sports. Riding the gnarliest wave or whatever else you're risking your neck doing. But you're a coward when it comes to life. To love. You're using these characters, these roles you've played, to hide behind and keep people from getting close to you."

The temptation to flee was strong, but he stood his ground and squared his shoulders instead. "That's not true."

"It's very true," she countered.

"You don't know what you're talking about." His voice sounded harsh. He didn't care. "I'm not a coward."

"Just calling it like I see it."

"So am I." Adam liked Megan. She knew him well, too well. He wasn't willing to take a leap of faith and trust things with her would work out because he knew they wouldn't. He would not put himself through that kind of hurt. "I like challenges, but not ones where I have no chance of succeeding."

"That's too bad. Sad, really." She blinked. Her eyes gleamed, but no tears fell. "If you aren't willing to risk yourself, your heart, you'll never succeed at what matters most in life. And you'll wind up...alone."

CHAPTER THIRTEEN

THREE days remained on the shoot. Adam had never been so damn miserable in his life. The only thing that kept him from sitting himself down at the local tavern night after night was the need to give this shoot his best effort. He needed to salvage something from this project. He doubted he'd be seeing an acting nomination now due to the tension on the set between him and Lane.

The actress used people and spat them out, but that didn't make her happy or feel less alone. Adam didn't want to end up like her, yet he felt so lonely, even surrounded by crew members. He'd wanted to avoid getting hurt, but he'd been hurting ever since Megan left.

His cell phone rang. The ring tone told him it was his mother. She was on an extended tour of Europe after her cruise. He hoped nothing was wrong. He hit Answer on his touch screen. "Mom?"

"Hi, Adam. I hope your shoot is going well."

Her cheerful tone lessened his concern. "I'll be back in L.A. in a couple of days. How's the vacation?"

"Wonderful." His mom sounded like she was smiling. "I met the most perfect man."

Adam grimaced. Not again. He prepared himself for what was no doubt the beginning of yet another end full of heartbreak and tears. "Who is he?"

Probably another in a long line of jerks.

"His name is Joseph Weber. We were seated at the same table for dinner. It wasn't love at first sight, but it didn't take me long to know I'd finally found my Mr. Right."

Yeah, Adam had heard that before. "I'm going to have the guy checked out."

"No need, dear, unless it'll make you feel better," his mother said. "Joseph owns his own security company in San Diego. He's an upright and law-abiding man."

Adam would still have him checked out. "At least you don't live too far away from him if you keep seeing him when you get home."

"Oh, we will." His mother sounded confident, but she usually did at the beginning of a new relationship. "I know I haven't been the best mother. I put my needs ahead of yours. But I always knew I'd find what we both needed. It took me longer to find than I thought it would, but I think you'll like Joseph as much as I do."

Adam's heart squeezed tight. His mom sounded like she was floating on air. He wasn't looking forward to her crashing and burning. "You'll have to introduce us."

He wanted to believe this time it would work out for her, even if the odds were slim to none.

"I'll call when I'm home," she said.

As soon as his mom said goodbye, he disconnected from the call. He tightened his grip on the phone. He didn't want his mom hurt again. It took everything in him not to reach out to the one person who he felt most comfortable with. The one person he wanted to see, to hear, more than anything.

Megan. He missed her.

Being with her lifted him up and made him stronger. When he was with her, he wanted to be a better man. She'd cared about him in a way no one had before, and he'd let her go.

Megan had been right.

He'd been a coward. Even his mother had been braver than him. She'd never given up trying to find Mr. Right. Even if she'd ended up with a lot of duds along the way. Whatever his mom kept searching for had to be pretty special if she kept risking her heart to find it.

Adam hadn't even tried. He'd been too scared of being hurt to risk it. He couldn't help himself. He'd held off everyone, even his own mom at times, because of what his dad had done all those years ago. Adam had even copied him by being an actor and a ladies' man. Someone who might disappoint, but could never be disappointed.

But Adam wasn't his father. He cared about people, about his mom, about Megan.

People changed. Megan had grown and changed before his eyes. She'd helped him do the same, too.

What was he doing?

He couldn't let his chance with Megan slip away because he was afraid. The risk of having her bail on him at some point was worth it to have her in his life now. The excitement of being together and trusting they could make it work would be like riding a wave or jumping out of an airplane. There weren't any guarantees, but that didn't mean it wouldn't work out.

Maybe it could. If it weren't too late.

Fatigue wore Megan down. She placed a pair of faded jeans, the only remaining item in her dresser, into the suitcase lying on her bed. She'd packed everything and wished she could pack away her broken heart, as well.

She could hardly sleep. Food didn't appeal to her. Nothing did.

Darn Adam Noble.

Megan was angry with him for not being willing to take a chance and at herself for falling for another man who couldn't love her back. Sadness gripped her heart like a fist and wouldn't let go. Emptiness, too, as if her insides had been hollowed out and left bare. Nothing, not even Rob offering to visit without Pru, had made Megan feel better.

But she wouldn't always feel this way. At least she hoped not. She rolled her suitcase to the front door. Everything she owned. Three boxes and two suitcases worth of stuff were ready to be loaded into her car. The furniture had come with the apartment, except for her little table. That would go in the car, too.

She glanced around the apartment. Even though she'd spent more time at the lot, and on location, this had become home, the one place—the first place—where she fit in and could be herself. No hiding. No pretending.

Not that she would ever go back to doing that again.

Lesson learned. Even if her family might not agree.

When she returned to Larkville in October for her father's celebration and a family reunion with her new half siblings, they would all have to accept it. Accept her. And even if they didn't... Well, she was a stronger, more confident woman now than when she left.

She double-checked the locks on the windows. She'd given her perishable food to Mrs. Hamilton downstairs, who still had out the vase from the flowers Adam had sent.

Thinking about him made her chest ache.

Best to forget everything to do with him. That was the only way to heal. She wasn't the first woman who'd had her heart broken. Unfortunately, she wouldn't be the last.

She'd cried enough. No more pity parties.

Someday she could look back on this and laugh at the time she went out with a famous movie star. Someday. Too bad that couldn't be today.

With a sigh, Megan loaded the table, suitcases and boxes into the back of her car. She decided to take one last look around the apartment to make sure she hadn't forgotten anything.

Inside, her footsteps echoed on the hardwood floor. It sounded as if she were in a cave. She recalled talking to a screenwriter while working on a one-day shoot as a stylist two weeks ago. He had told her about the Writer's Journey, a method used to plot scripts. Megan had accepted the call to adventure when she took the internship. Now she wanted out of the innermost cave. The rest of her life was waiting for her. And maybe, just maybe, she would find the elixir—the treasure—to have made this journey worthwhile.

Best get finished with this portion so she could move on to what came next. Her plans hadn't turned out like she expected, but she was coming to realize that was okay.

She double-checked the closet, the bathroom and the small kitchen. All the drawers and cupboards were empty. Time to go.

"You're leaving."

The sound of Adam's voice sent a chill down her spine. Every nerve ending stood to attention. Once again, a million and one thoughts ran through her head. She focused on one— *don't lose it.*

Slowly, she faced him. "Yes, I am."

Adam stood four feet away from her. His hair was damp, as if he'd gone for a swim or showered recently. He wore a pair of board shirts and a faded T-shirt.

So handsome. Gorgeous. But looks didn't make a man.

Whether on the set or off it, Adam played roles. She wasn't sure who the real man was now. Too bad because she'd liked the Adam she'd gotten to know on set, but for all she knew he was as make-believe as the character he was playing in the movie.

She raised her chin. "What do you want?"

His gaze met hers. "You."

The air rushed from her lungs. She didn't know what to say.

He took a step toward her.

Self-preservation made her back away from him. He was too handsome, too charming. She couldn't allow herself to be swayed by him. That had happened twice already. "I have to go."

"Where?"

"Portland, Oregon."

"The beautiful Pacific Northwest."

"I hear it's very green and rains a lot," she said. "I was of-fered a job on a shoot there. Someone heard about me from

Hugh Wilstead. Imagine that. The man whose fiancée had me fired."

"It's funny how things work in this town."

"No kidding," she agreed. "I tried to find a position on my own, but kept coming up empty even with Eva as a reference. Not enough experience was the standard line I kept hearing, if I heard anything at all."

Adam took a step closer. "Someone must have called in a favor."

"I'm just happy for the chance." Megan didn't know why she was telling him all this. She needed to shut up. He'd made his choice. She'd made hers. She stared down her nose at him. "Not that it matters to you."

"But it does."

Huh? Megan started to speak, then stopped herself. She wasn't sure how to respond. Or if she should.

Adam crossed the distance between them in two long strides. "I'm sorry, Megan. I was an idiot for the way I acted at the airport."

Emotion swirled through her. Part of Megan wanted to throw herself into Adam's arms and kiss him. The other part wanted to see him on his knees groveling at her feet.

He touched the side of her face. "I want to make it up to you. I want us to be together."

Warmth flowed through her. His words filled her heart with hope. She cared about him. She wanted to be with him.

But no matter how she might want to believe what he said was true, Megan didn't dare. He'd said it himself. He wasn't the right man for her. They'd already played this scene and it hadn't ended well. She looked away. "I have to go."

"I'm not talking about a fling," Adam said. "I'm talking long-term."

Her gaze jerked up to his. "You don't do long-term."

"I haven't," he admitted. "That doesn't mean I can't. Forever with you sounds awesome to me."

Her mouth gaped. She closed it. His words wouldn't let the hope in her heart die.

"I miss you, Megan. I don't want to lose you."

She was tempted. Oh, how she was tempted. But that road would only lead her to where she was now...brokenhearted.

Megan moved past him. Getting far away from him was her smartest move at the moment. "I'm sure you'll find someone else on the set to keep you company. If you haven't already."

"I love you."

She froze. Her shoes felt as if they'd been glued to the floor.

"I love you, Megan Calhoun," Adam said. "I understand why you're upset. If you want to leave, go. I don't blame you. But if there's a part of you who wants to take a chance on a risky guy like me, here I am. I'm yours."

Her pulse rocketed out of control.

His gaze implored her. "You were dead-on about me playing roles. But not with you. It was only when I got scared, realizing how close we'd gotten, that I wasn't myself. It's what I did when I was a kid to survive. But you showed me it could be different. I could be myself. I want to be with you, Megan. I'm willing to do whatever it takes to keep you in my life."

Her heart pounded so loudly she was sure people in the next apartment could hear it. She stared at Adam with a mix of surprise, affection and respect. The sincerity in his eyes and the way he stumbled over his words made her believe he was telling the truth.

He loved her.

Fireworks exploded inside her. "I love you, too."

Adam pulled her toward him. He lowered his mouth to hers and kissed her firmly on the lips. His arms wrapped around her. She went willingly, eagerly. She melted against him, allowing his kiss to consume her. This was where she belonged.

"I want to spend the rest of my life with you." He ran the side of his finger along her jaw. "But first I want you to go after your dreams."

The love in his eyes matched the way she felt. "They're already coming true."

He removed something from his pocket—a ring box.

The air rushed from her lungs.

"This is a promise ring. I don't want you to feel rushed or any pressure. But I promise—" he slid it on the ring finger of her left hand "—when you're ready, I'll replace this with an engagement ring."

She stared at the silver ring. The diamond sparkled. She couldn't imagine any engagement ring being more beautiful.

"It's…" Megan struggled to find the perfect word. "Stunning."

He kissed her hand. "Not as stunning as you."

She studied him. "Are you sure about this?"

"I'm not sure what the future will hold," he admitted. "But I'm sure I want you in it. I'm committed to making this work."

That was good enough for her. "A part of me wishes I didn't have to go to Portland now."

"Why? There's so much to do there—climbing, skydiving, waterskiing, year-round skiing on Mount Hood."

His daredevil ways hadn't changed. She smiled. "Let me guess, you want to BASE jump off Mount Hood?"

"No," he admitted. "But I have in mind a few adventures for us. Ones we can do and experience together to create memories."

"Too bad we'll have to wait to do those things until we're together."

Mischief gleamed in his eyes. "My shoot is in Portland, too."

Megan didn't know how he'd managed that, and she didn't care. They were going to be together. That was what mattered. She rose on her tiptoes and kissed Adam on the lips, hard.

"And I have an adventure for us…in Larkville." She had no idea what it would be like to bring him home, but she had a feeling it wouldn't be bad. "We're celebrating my dad's life at the annual Fall Festival in October. My entire family will be there, including my half siblings. I'd love it if you would go with me."

"I'm in." Adam didn't hesitate. "I can't wait to meet your brothers and sister."

"*Sisters,* remember—I have a brand-new one!" Megan smiled a bit nervously. Adam looked at her and grinned.

"It doesn't matter how many sisters you have, you'll always stand out."

Megan blushed. "Well, you're the one who's helped me to stop hiding and start having adventures!"

"And the lessons have only just begun."

He kissed her again, a kiss worthy of a Viewers' Choice Award for Best Kiss. Or maybe the MTV Movie Awards gave out that one. Either way, Megan knew she and Adam were the real winners no matter what happened after the screen faded to black.

Happily ever after. Sounded like a perfect ending to her. She had a feeling Adam would agree.

* * * * *

COMING NEXT MONTH from Harlequin® Romance
AVAILABLE NOVEMBER 27, 2012

#4351 SINGLE DAD'S HOLIDAY WEDDING
Rocky Mountain Brides
Patricia Thayer
Jace is going to prove to new boss Lori who's the real boss. Is this the season for second chances?

#4352 THE SECRET THAT CHANGED EVERYTHING
The Larkville Legacy
Lucy Gordon
Charlotte and Lucio share one intensely passionate night together—a night that will affect them more than they could possibly imagine...

#4353 MISTLETOE KISSES WITH THE BILLIONAIRE
Holiday Miracles
Shirley Jump
Back in her small hometown for Christmas, can Grace find happiness the second time around with her ex-boyfriend JC?

#4354 HER OUTBACK RESCUER
Journey Through the Outback
Marion Lennox
For billionaire Hugo, ex-ballerina Amy threatens to derail his icy cool. But with no time for distractions, will he succumb to her charms?

#4355 BABY UNDER THE CHRISTMAS TREE
Teresa Carpenter
When Max's ex abandons their son, Elle steps in to help. This Christmas, the best gift of all is family!

#4356 THE NANNY WHO SAVED CHRISTMAS
Michelle Douglas
This Christmas, nanny Nicola is determined to make a difference. Cade and his little daughters are the perfect place to start...

You can find more information on upcoming Harlequin® titles, free excerpts and more at www.Harlequin.com.

HRCNM1112

*Is the Santina-Jackson royal fairy-tale engagement
too good to be true?*

*Read on for a sneak peek of
PLAYING THE ROYAL GAME by USA TODAY
bestselling author Carol Marinelli.*

* * *

"I HAVE also spoken to my parents."

"They've heard?"

"They were the ones who alerted me!" Alex said. "We
have aides who monitor the press and the news constantly."
Did she not understand he had been up all night dealing
with this? "I am waiting for the palace to ring—to see how
we will respond."

She couldn't think, her head was spinning in so many
directions and Alex's presence wasn't exactly calming—
not just his tension, not just the impossible situation, but
the sight of him in her kitchen, the memory of his kiss. That
alone would have kept her thoughts occupied for days on
end, but to have to deal with all this, too…. And now the
doorbell was ringing. He followed her as she went to hit the
display button.

"It's my dad." She was actually a bit relieved to see him.
"He'll know what to do, how to handle—"

"I thought you hated scandal," Alex interrupted.

"We'll just say—"

"I don't think you understand." Again he interrupted
her and there was no trace of the man she had met yesterday; instead she faced not the man but the might of

Crown Prince Alessandro Santina. "There is no question that you will go through with this."

"You can't force me." She gave a nervous laugh. "We both know that yesterday was a mistake." She could hear the doorbell ringing. She went to press the intercom but his hand halted her, caught her by the wrist. She shot him the same look she had yesterday, the one that should warn him away, except this morning it did not work.

"You agreed to this, Allegra, the money is sitting in your account." He looked down at the paper. "Of course, we could tell the truth…" He gave a dismissive shrug. "I'm sure they have photos of later."

"It was just a kiss…."

"An expensive kiss," Alex said. "I wonder what the papers would make of it if they found out I bought your services yesterday."

"You wouldn't." She could see it now, could see the horrific headlines—she, Allegra, in the spotlight, but for shameful reasons.

"Oh, Allegra," he said softly but without endearment. "Absolutely I would. It's far too late to change your mind."

* * *

Pick up PLAYING THE ROYAL GAME by Carol Marinelli on November 13, 2012, from Harlequin® Presents®.